Roads to Hell

A Novel By
Rory Macleod

Published 2010 by arima publishing
www.arimapublishing.com

ISBN 978 1 84549 438 4
© Rory Macleod 2010

Printed and bound in the United Kingdom

Typeset in Garamond 11/14

Swirl is an imprint of arima publishing.

arima publishing
ASK House, Northgate Avenue
Bury St Edmunds, Suffolk IP32 6BB
t: (+44) 01284 700321
www.arimapublishing.com

Part One: Allies

Why should Hell be free of love?
Every land must know love, even the dead must burn
With the fires that Venus kindles.
 – Claudian

1.   The Gate

I seem to be busier these days at the Gate. The tube trains come in
packed with people. Old folk by and large of course, but most mornings I
find one or two squaddies who step out in desert camouflage with their
kitbags in their hands. My job is to be the greeter, like the redcoat in a
Butlins holiday camp, and put them at their ease, explain how things work
here. I've been around a long time and I know the ropes. The crowd mills
about on the tube platform and then heads for the escalator. The old
souls hang on to the rail but the squaddies stride up decisively,
determined to get to the top and find out exactly what's going on. I
introduce myself when they are through the turnstiles and I am always
happy to see their faces light up in recognition at seeing an officer.
Generally they salute me but I tell them that it isn't necessary here. I take
them to the Naafi over the way and give them a cup of tea and a slice of
toast and explain the situation. They don't take it in at all, I can see that. It
took me quite a time, I tell them.

'My name is Deeds, but you can call me Dodo,' I say. They find that
odd but I explain that in my day everybody I knew had a nickname. They
sip their tea and listen as I explain how I came to be called 'Dodo'. One
summer afternoon, I tell them, I was fielding at a school cricket match. I
heard the snick as the ball left the bat and watched it soar through the air
and drop towards me. I held out my hands for the catch but the ball
struck me on the temple. One moment I was waiting to catch the ball and
the next I was lying on the grass staring at a sky full of stars. Two figures
bent over me. They look like foreigners, I thought. The man had a black
beard and a king's crown like tinsel and a sceptre which he used to jab at
my wound so my head hurt. The woman wore a dress of pale violet
gathered tightly around her waist. She knelt over me and as she smiled
her eyes widened so I saw the whites of her eyes all around the green

irises. I could smell her perfume of attar of roses.

'I've never forgotten that scent,' I say. What I don't say is that every day on the Gate, I wait to smell it again. It can't be long now, it really can't. Their eyes are darting about and I resume my story.

The woman touched my lips with her finger and then she looked at her companion and shook her head. A scowl passed across the man's bearded face and he turned away. She leaned over me again before following and kissed the mark. I tried to get up so I could see where they were going.

'Deeds is dead! Dead as a dodo!' shouted the boys as they gathered round where I was lying on the grass but I recovered after they carried me to the sanatorium. The nickname stuck. I show the squaddie the round scar on my temple.

As I walk them over to their quarters I always ask the boys how they got to be here. Most of the time they don't remember. They were walking down a hot dusty village street or riding in a vehicle or crouched behind a wall with their mates, and that is the last thing they recall. But a while back I met a young man, an officer in intelligence, who could tell me his whole story. He had been in a boat going under a bridge and suddenly there was a burst of fire from somebody on the bridge above and he had been blinded.

'I was twenty-four years old,' he said.

'Same age as me,' I responded. I've been twenty-four for a long time.

When he got out of hospital, he told me, he killed himself with an overdose of sleeping pills. He had been to university and done a lot of thinking.

'It was a war for oil,' he said. 'Think we would have attacked them if they'd been growing cabbages? Not bloody likely.'

He was quite upset and to calm him down I told him about my war, the good war. But he said my idea it was fought by good folks against bad folks was just a Hollywood version of history.

'Stalin was your ally. He was just as evil as Hitler who was your enemy.'

'Uncle Joe and the Russians? They were good people,' I replied.

'Both were evil men. Hitler killed his millions and Stalin his tens of millions.'

I didn't know much about Stalin, and the young man convinced me I had to let go of looking at my war as a good war. It has been immensely comforting to me but I see now its time is past. He was full of irony. He told me his soldiers didn't believe in good wars any more. And now I understand that my war, the second world war, was really the first world war for oil.

'Nineteen forty-three was a different world, Dodo, I'll grant you that,' said the blind man. 'Your world was full of children not the old, of white people versus everybody else. But it was an oil war all the same. Listen. Hitler tried to force his way through Egypt to the oil fields of Arabia but he failed, and the Saudis stayed in the pockets of the Americans. We held Palestine and seized the oil in Iraq. Iraq, Dodo. Now do you understand? Your war was an oil war.'

He's right about things having changed. For instance, over the years I've watched the people on the Gate get fatter and fatter. In England in my time there were as many words for thin (slim, lanky, willowy, lean, skinny, gaunt) as these young squaddies use for fat (large, heavy, strong, plump, stout, obese). I'm out of date. America to me means chocolate bars and bubble gum and I remember when British families ate whale meat sandwiches and dreamed of drinking Vimto. I don't understand climate change or computers at all.

'When this country,' the young man continued, and I wondered for a moment whether to correct him but then thought – he'll find out soon enough. 'When this country was alive as some of the casualties on my ward were alive, just kept going on morphine and blood - when things were entirely different from the way they are nowadays but people were the same – you lot fought a world war for oil. It's still going on. It's why I'm here, just like you.'

He set me to thinking again about the last year of my life, when I never got to be more than twenty-four years old. Perhaps I should say dreaming rather than thinking, for I've always been able to remember my dreams, so that when I dream I re-enter a dream world and the dreams I had when I was a child are as real to me as what I am dreaming at that moment. Over the years I've met most of the people I knew during the war. They've all moved on now. Even Scuffy, who hung around longer than anybody, has moved on. But I know I'm not ready yet.

Yesterday I was on duty at the Gate as usual. The crowd got off the tube and trudged over to the escalators. A tiny elderly lady in a faded kimono was left behind on the platform. Suddenly I heard the clatter of boots on the stairs and a young soldier in Japanese uniform from the Pacific war ran up to her shouting a name. He picked her up and whirled about with her in his arms and when they stopped – I'm not pulling your leg, I really saw it happen- when he put her down it was as though a faded old flower had opened out in bloom again. She was young and beautiful and still wearing her kimono but now its colours were as bright as a summer's day. What the old man told me in the city under the ground is really true. There is love in hell.

So I'm still waiting for her. Meanwhile let me tell you my story.

2.   July 1943

'War?' I replied. 'You want to know about war, Dougie? Only the dead could tell us about war, the real truth of war. And as for me,' I added as I turned back to the map, 'I'm in no hurry to learn.'

At Goubrine Two the fuel had arrived on the morning before the attack. Tankers went from aircraft to aircraft and men wearing goggles and with scarves wrapped around their faces stood below the metal wings and held the fuel lines as the kerosene was pumped in. The desert wind swept away the stink of fuel as it evaporated in the intense heat. Jeeps and trucks criss-crossed the airstrip and a thick white dust that tasted of salt and sand rose over everything. The wooden gliders were lined up behind the aircraft like an assembly line and the ground crews wore gloves as they connected the tow ropes covered with sticky melting tar. It was late afternoon and the sun sank behind the haze. Aircrews took off the covers that protected the engines and the perspex canopies of the cockpits and polished the aircraft to reduce wind resistance, and the jeeps with portable generators behind them moved from machine to machine jump-starting the motors.

'Here are the four points along the coast,' Peter resumed, pointing to the map that was spread out against the side of his Albemarle aeroplane. 'Point D is where I release your glider. We'll talk on the intercom but if that fails I will flash an Aldis lamp from the aircraft when you need to cast off. You have to glide four miles from the release point to the bridge.'

Dougie and Charlie Coombs worked on the landing. They would put on the airbrakes when they saw the bridge over the canal. It was vital the Horsa wasn't travelling at over 90 miles per hour or the jacks on the wings that used compressed air to put up the spoilers would tear away.

'At an angle of sixty degrees it will feel like we're flying right into the ground. We'll have to wash out the speed just before the airbrakes come on,' Charlie told me. 'We'll lift the nose just before landing,' said Dougie, 'and put on the wheel brakes. With the callipers clamped to the insides of the two rear wheels the Horsa will stop in under a hundred yards. Don't worry.'

'Smith opens the fuselage doors, gets the men out and we head for the bridge,' I agreed. I felt confident when I listened to the two burly sergeants and their jargon but I knew about war and after I walked away I crouched down in the salt dust and put my head between my knees. I spent the last hours at Goubrine lying on my bed trying to sleep and composing a letter to Bella that I did not write. Why? Because I was frightened of telling her I might die. So I drank water and sweated and kept my bowels in check. A stiff wind lashed against the sides of the tent.

My soldiers put on their equipment in the sandstorm. There wasn't enough room in the tents so they stood outside with their backs to the wind. Each man carried a rifle, ammunition, gas mask, helmet, grenades, spade and sandbags for entrenching, water bottle and two days of emergency rations. They tied them onto their bodies with webbing and rope. Sergeant Smith walked around checking the loads then popped his head inside the tent to report.

'When I was a nipper on the Somme,' he said, 'I never had to carry as much kit as these lads.'

Bending over the holes dug into the salt floor to protect the Benghazi cookers from the wind, the soldiers brewed a last cup of tea and the sergeant put a tot of rum into each mug. I watched my platoon stepping over the tow ropes and round the piles of gear as they moved towards the glider door. The propellers were turning faster, whipping up the sand so the men coughed and choked and they reached out and took hold of the shoulder of the man in front for support. A few gazed around but the dust storm was as thick as a cloud of gas. Smith pushed each man inside until all were strapped in on two long rows on the wooden benches, then I got in last and locked the door shut. I could hardly turn around in the darkness inside the fuselage. The glider was as crowded as an assembly trench in the minutes before the big push.

Each unit of three tugs took off at thirty second intervals and there was a gap of one minute before the next three. The tugs formed a V, and circled the aerodrome at a thousand feet until a stepped-up V of nine planes had formed. Then they headed out over the sea.

This was our plan but Peter had a headache with his Albemarle immediately he had taken off. The starboard engine lost power and he circled back over Goubrine ready for an emergency landing before it righted itself. We lost contact with the other aircraft. Over the Malta beacon we saw the convoy of tugs and gliders ahead but we couldn't catch up and he told Dougie he was pushing the aircraft up to 5,000 feet.

'With this wind you'll need the extra height,' he bellowed through the intercom. 'And I'm going to take you two miles nearer the target before I release you. There's some flak coming up from the coast ahead.'

I stood behind Dougie and Charlie, who were taking it in turns to fly the Horsa. The job was hard because the glider yawed from side to side behind the tug in an unpredictable way and if nothing was done the see-saw motion could eventually turn the aircraft over. The pilot had constantly to touch the ailerons to keep the Horsa level, and at the same time he could not allow the towrope to get slack or the glider to rise too high above the tug. But they were both strong men. Dougie had told me he was a bricklayer in civvy street and Charlie was an Army regular who had boxed for his battalion in India.

We could see the coast and the burning city clearly below. Peter flew along the coastline and gave Dougie the points on the map as he passed them. One minute after point D he told him to release, climbed and turned for home. After Dougie cast off we lost height and the fires lit up the horizon. We circled south over the city as we looked for the bridge over the main road to the invasion beaches, where the river and canal flowed together into the harbour. The landing zone was nearby. Charlie flew the Horsa as we had agreed at Goubrine. Everything was going according to plan.

'There's the landing zone,' called out Charlie and took the Horsa down a bit more. He lined up for the final descent. Some flak was bursting but it seemed to be well above us. He glanced over and Dougie gave him the thumbs-up sign. Charlie leaned towards the central column to put the airbrakes on. The glider jerked to one side and I winced and instinctively shut my eyes. When I opened them again there was a hole in the other side of the cockpit where Charlie had been sitting. His seat was still there but the straps were hanging loose and Charlie Coombs was gone. The slipstream was tearing at everything. I could see the landing zone, a small field that ran up against the side of the canal.

'Hundred and ten,' shouted Dougie, checking his airspeed. 'I'm going too fast. I'll rip the jacks off the wings if I put the airbrakes on now. Lift the nose.' He pulled back on his control column. The airspeed was dropping and he pushed on the lever to engage the airbrakes. There was a hiss as compressed air rushed out of the cylinder bolted to the floor and into the jacks attached to the wings. The Horsa's nose tilted steeply down and I lost my balance. I fell onto the central column and rolled towards the hole on Charlie's half of the cockpit. The ground came up rapidly to meet us. Dougie waited until the last moment then lifted the nose. The glider touched down almost perfectly and he pushed the lever to put on the wheel brakes. The lever moved easily. Too easily, I thought and glanced at the floor. The second bottle of compressed air was rolling around loosely at my feet.

The Horsa glider was moving too fast across the field. Impersonal forces were free to work out the manner in which it would come to a complete stop. The friction of the air against the wings and fuselage was having an effect. More importantly, the friction of the soil was acting on the rubber of the wheels. Given enough distance, the energy the glider carried in its forward motion would be turned by this friction into heat and it would gradually slow. Indeed this was already happening – but not fast enough. The glider reached the earth bank after six seconds. Its wooden nose hit the bank and the metal bolts binding the floor of the cockpit to the rest of the glider sheared. The nose tilted up. Dougie slammed against his restraining straps.

The two sergeants and their helpers at Mascara had built my Horsa well. Each section held. The wings shuddered but they stayed attached to the fuselage. The triangular frames of metal holding the wheels came through the wooden sides. They missed the men who had been thrown forward by the impact and buried themselves in the underside of the wings. The glider stopped moving. But the ropes tying down the Bangalore torpedo at the rear of the fuselage had not been tightened. The torpedo, a metal cylinder ten feet long with explosives inside, broke loose under the strain. It slid along the floor between the jerking legs of the men and blew up inside Dougie's cockpit. The blast killed everybody on board, but the airframe held together and the wreck of the wooden glider smoked in the thin moonlight.

3.   March

But I am rushing ahead. Let me go back in time a few months to the day of my twenty-fourth birthday, so I can explain how I came to be inside that glider. It was early morning at the little port of Tabarka on the Tunisian coastline and I was helping bury a friend. The Arab porters wheeled the trolley across the road from the field hospital. In the cemetery overlooking the sea I threw a handful of soil into the grave and while the rest of the burial party got the trucks ready for the outing I walked down to the beach. The sky was a brilliant blue and the sea was still foaming after the storm. I sat down on a rock and watched the waves quietly, thinking about the sea nymphs that the ancients had believed in and Thetis the mother of Achilles doomed to die in battle. On the horizon I could see a plume of smoke.

Is it an aircraft in trouble? No, it's not moving, I decided. Perhaps the smoke comes from mount Etna.

In those days I was tall and fair with a lick of hair that flopped over my forehead and eyes that were grey with flecks of hazel in them – very English eyes, slightly watery, my mother used to say. I was popular with the hospital nurses. They were glad to make friends with a handsome man who was clearly going to live. Before Jonny died from blood poisoning I had fucked a South African nurse in the lavatories. Her name was Barbara and she had short blonde hair that I loved to twist in my hands. She leaned against the door of the stall to keep it shut and I pulled down her slacks. After, she was angry that I had ejaculated inside her and grabbed the harsh lavatory paper to wipe off the semen as it dripped onto her panties.

Now Barbara was shouting at me from the road. 'Wake up Dodo!' she called in her high-pitched Durban voice, 'the lorries are ready. We don't want to keep the piccanies waiting.'

The war had moved away from the little seaside resort and as the weather got warmer some of the nurses wanted to explore the countryside. Over the hills was a ruined Roman city famous for its mosaics. The major in charge of transport organised a couple of trucks – back then they were called lorries –for nurses and patients to go there and stay the night, but first we would get a morning's sport doing some pig-sticking. The town of Tabarka lay on the other bank of the river from the hospital, a quiet place with colonial buildings along the corniche and a tree-lined square where we parked across from the bakery. The men bought some loaves and swapped tins of Bengal Lancer cigarettes for the local arak liquor. Turning inland the road ran through villages of dried mud and brick, each one with a mosque and a minaret made out of steel girders, before it wound up hairpin bends into an oak forest. I braced myself against the side of the cab because the wound in my leg, which had almost healed, was hurting.

The gamekeepers were waiting for us at the head of the valley and we drove along a dirt track that ran far above the water of a long narrow lake. Stones from the tyres fell into the lake as the trucks passed. When the going got worse we went on by foot, heading up the steep hill and at the top we lay about on the narrow path eating tangerines. Some keepers only had spears: steel blades tied onto the ends of long sticks. The headman was armed with a 16-bore shotgun of great age. Around his waist he wore a bandolier of cartridges. They were used ones but he extracted the metal cap, put in a match head and tapped the cap straight. The cartridges were slow to take fire but effective if the follow-through was correct. I was given an Italian submachine gun of smaller calibre than a tommy gun but lighter and easier to handle.

The pig-sticking party were several thousand feet up and we had a glorious view in the faultless clear air. On the other side of the valley stood hills covered with the same vivid green woods. Eagles were soaring over the top of our hill: big birds with buff backs and wings and white bellies. The beaters lined up along the crest of the hill and drove the pigs towards us. They were going fast and moved silently for such big beasts. Soon after the beaters had started I heard a crash in the undergrowth, followed by a shot, then more crashing. The beaters drew near and there was a good deal of noise when I heard something moving in the undergrowth in front of me. An enormous boar jumped over the path about ten yards away and went tumbling into the thicket below. I emptied a 40-round magazine into the bushes but heard the noise as it made its way down the steep slope long after the magazine was empty.

For the next drive we all stood in a line up and down the hill. The end of the line was in a grassy meadow studded with big brown bulbs just sprouting thick leaves. Butterflies flitted about, mostly ones I knew: Red Admirals, Brimstones, some Wood Whites I had not seen in Africa before and of course a good many Painted Ladies. It was a long distance for such delicate insects to migrate, I thought. Fishermen would sometimes glimpse clouds of butterflies resting from their journey on the surface of the waters, a shimmering patch of colours. I recalled the Painted Ladies in my parents' garden on the summer evening when I had kissed a girl for the first time and been surprised when she put her tongue into my mouth. Earlier that day Papa had called me into his study and told me he could not afford to send his son to university. I caught a Painted Lady in my hands and showed it to Laura before I repeated what he said about going out to India.

After a short wait one dog started giving tongue in the distance as it chased a boar. The sound came straight towards me but stopped just out of sight in a thicket. I could hear the boar grunting and I trained my gun on the spot where I expected it to emerge. The bushes parted and the beast came straight at me. I pulled the trigger but nothing happened and the boar headed past me down the meadow, hotly pursued by the dog.

The dog was well-trained and succeeded in turning the pig back. It tried to cross the path further up and was killed with a single shot by a rifle. She was a sow, about two years old with thick black hair and a powerful smell. I examined my weapon and realised the magazine was still empty. I've got the shells in my pockets to reload but I must be suffering from concussion, I thought. The doctors said it could take months to pass.

Two of the beaters gutted the pig with a table-knife. They had to use a rock to get through the bone. An old man had been carrying a basket and he collected all the offal. I watched and decided the beaters, piccanies or wogs as I called them then, were the most miserable specimens of humanity I had ever seen with the filthy blankets which they twisted round their bodies. By this time the sun was getting high in the sky and we descended the hill with the pig on a pole. The man with the offal in the basket went in front, but the smell fouled the air beyond all endurance and we sent him back to join the pig. The leaves of the shrubs, which had smelt unpleasant in the morning, now gave off a rather pleasant, exotic scent. It was dead still with not a breath of wind and the noises made by the farmers and shepherds had died away with the coming of the heat. We passed a few of them riding their scruffy donkeys on our way back to drink tea at the truck.

By the time we had met up with the nurses and come over the hills to the river the sun was setting. We stopped by a grey concrete pillbox pitted with shrapnel marks that guarded the approaches to the bridge. It was a good place for an ambush and a tank lay like a drunk in the ditch next to the pillbox, its long barrel pointing at the sky. In a field nearby stood a group of wooden crosses. I walked past them to where the muddy water flowed slowly between reeds. The mist lay over the further bank and I could just make out the shape of a boat. As I watched the boat moved out into the river and as it reached the bank downstream from where I stood a second figure appeared from the reeds with a sheep on his back and passed it to the man in the boat. The sheep had its feet tied and lay quietly in the bottom as three more sheep were lifted in. When the boat was full the man punted it lightly back across the river and lifted the sheep out and cut the ropes so they could run free. The sheep wandered off into the mist.

At the ruined city we parked next to the museum. The nurses put up camp beds between the display cases and I lay down for a few minutes to rest my leg. I went outside where a fire was burning in the courtyard and drank a mug of tea laced with arak. Barbara was on the other side of the fire laughing with her friends. The liquor blended well with condensed milk and sugar and I tilted my head back to catch the last few drops. Above my head ran the constellations with the jagged white gash of the Milky Way across the middle.

Looks just like a hospital bandage, I thought, just like the bandage across my head wound.

4. Marshal Foch

The next morning all I could see of the site was a dusty space of low stone walls and beyond a little town with the rubble of a fort on a knoll. The scrubland rose to meet the bare hills above. I ducked behind the shelter of a wall and flicked on my Zippo to light a cigarette. Peering into a hole I realised the magic of the place was underground. Below was a mosaic floor with a portico around it. I climbed down the steps and stood at one side of the floor, which was made up of thousands of small coloured stones arranged into a picture of a young man sitting on a rock. In his hands he held a lyre made from two curved horns and his mouth was open as though he was singing. A soft cap covered his hair and he wore a red cloak.

The young man was surrounded by animals. On one side the beasts were sitting or standing peaceably. But on the other wild boars, a spotted leopard and a lioness bared their teeth. From the branch of a tree a crow looked on with a sardonic air as though he knew what was going to happen next. Above the young man's head was a caption. The indecipherable words added to the sinister feeling the scene conveyed.

I looked at the metal sign. It read, 'Orpheus and the wild animals. The script is ancient Etruscan and has not been deciphered. It may represent a cult of the dead, of immortality and the underworld.'

A voice behind me said, 'You like the joke?'

In the shade of the portico a short man aged about fifty years stood with arms folded. His grey hair was cut straight across the top of his skull and he was dressed in a neat old blue jacket with dark trousers. The outfit gave him a military air but it was rubbed bare at the elbows and knees.

'I'm sorry?'

'The joke,' repeated the man and pointed with a long bony finger.

I saw that one of the t's of 'immortality' had been scratched out.

'A cult of immorality, you see,' the man added. 'But the bit about the underworld is misleading. It's true Orpheus went down to Hell to rescue his wife but he couldn't bring her back. It isn't easy to do. Afterwards he was torn apart by wild animals.'

I looked at the floor again.

'I wouldn't know,' I said.

The man seemed unconcerned by his failure to start a conversation. He turned away and I climbed into the light again and walked across to where a crowd of soldiers and nurses was gathered around the statue of a nude girl. One arm and part of her chin were missing and she had lifted a leg gracefully to tie on a tiny sandal hanging from her toes. Barbara saw me and grinned before stubbing her cigarette out on the statue's nose.

'This one is Venus rising from the waves,' said the man with the military air, who had followed me upstairs. He moved his head back and forth as though to indicate the endlessness of the dusty waste around us.

'Here it is a bit ridiculous. She is rising from the earth into the desert as you see.'

He looks like one of those old French generals, I thought, like Marshal Foch perhaps. But this Marshal Foch is terribly thin. His eyes are almost popping out of his face and his cheeks are hollow.

'Are you an archaeologist?' I asked.

The man shook his head. 'I am the curator of the site and earn a few pennies. Let me show you something considerably more interesting, which a connoisseur like you will appreciate.'

Dirty pictures, I reckoned as Marshal Foch limped away without looking to see if he was being followed. He pushed his way between two acacia bushes and held them apart.

'I see that you too are a victim of war,' he said as I passed by. 'I received my wound in the service of France. For many years it did not bother me but now I am old it is catching up. Where were you hurt?'

'At Mareth. At the Mareth Line.'

I close my eyes and see a snake of men marching in the moonlight. Flares shoot up and arc to show an expanse of desert. The soldiers climb a long slope in single file. On the other side I can't see more than a few yards and the noise of gunfire overwhelms me. I give the word to move forward and the men stumble down the bank into the wadi where the moonlight glints on the water. What scares me are the S-mines that spring up when you step on them and explode at the height of your crotch. Almost immediately I see a flash and hear a screech as somebody treads on a mine.

We cross the stream and stumble into a ditch dragging the wounded with us. Now British tanks roll into the wadi. A tank bogs down in the mud near where we are hiding. Enemy searchlights are searching for the attackers. I can hear again the sound of the shells bursting and soldiers screaming.

Someone is singing at the top of his voice. First one man and then others join in. It is the song of the local football side back home:

They called on me to sang a song
So I sang 'em 'Paddy Fagan'
I danced a jig and I swung me twig
The day I went to Blaydon'.

The sergeant at my side clambers up the ditch and the troops follow him forward into the gunfire, singing the chorus to the song. I find I am following too.

I opened my eyes and realised I had been singing aloud. The Marshal was rubbing his moustache as he said, 'Yes, we too had our songs in the trenches. This is the spot.' He brushed away leaves, showing a trap door with a handle set into the ground and I helped him tug at the trap. The door sighed and lifted up so suddenly that we nearly fell into the darkness below.

5.   Proserpine

We walked down a stairway cut into the stone and Marshal Foch came back into the square of light with an oil lamp. Lighting it with my Zippo he said, 'The archaeologists went back to Paris. It has not been opened since last autumn just before the Germans came. But look at this.' He placed the lamp on the ground and I saw a face staring back at me, a dark face with a black beard. The figure was holding a spear and sitting on a chair made out of bones.

'We are standing in the villa of Pluto, and here is Pluto himself, the lord of ghosts. Around him are shades without number.' He pointed at rows of figures, uncertain in the light of the lamp.

'Pluto rules a third of the universe but he is alone in it, the only living creature. He wants a wife. He wants to be loved. Why shouldn't there be love in hell?'

Marshal Foch halted again and got down on his hands and knees. I knocked over a bucket which clanked away into the blackness as I looked over his shoulder. He uncovered a mosaic full of colour - blue stones of lapis lazuli, fragments of green glass like emeralds and pieces of white marble.

'This map represents the universe,' said the Marshal as the light from the lamp played on his face with its beaky nose and shadows below the eyes. 'Above are the heavens where Jupiter reigns in splendour, below is the ocean. Can you see the seaweed on the rocks? Are you surprised that Pluto is so angry when he sees what his brothers have taken?'

He moved more of the sacking aside to reveal a yellow landscape.

'How cunningly she has woven the world! The desert is where we are, here in the middle, and to north and south the green lands. Beyond are the lands of snow, ultima Thule.' He laughed a little crazily.

I was losing the thread of all this so I asked, 'She? Who is she?'

'The daughter of Jupiter. Haven't you noticed her?' He lifted the lamp and I saw the map was a tapestry in the lap of a young woman. Her hair was deep black, almost purple in colour, and her large green eyes stared at me.

'Look where she is pointing.'

I followed the old man's extended finger. In the middle of the sea was a tiny triangle of mosaic stones, no more than six or seven, with one black or dark-blue one in the middle.

'Trinacria, the three-cornered island,' the marshal said in a dreamy voice, quite unlike his usual rasp. 'This is the maiden Proserpine or Persephone as the Greeks called her. Her mother Ceres was the goddess of the harvest and Sicily is where her mother has hidden her. But uncle Pluto will soon steal her away. And the black spot? Where the rape will happen. At Etna perhaps, or lake Pergusa, or the fountain of Ciane. There are many candidates in the legend.'

He broke off and turned out the light. 'I heard a noise outside,' he whispered as he climbed the steps and closed the trap door.

'The town is not as peaceful as it was before the Germans came. Young soldiers, red and sunburned, nervous, looking for diesel for the vehicles. My friend Yusuf owned the store. Somebody said that he was hiding fuel. So they shot him and his son in the square. Now an Arab family runs the shop. The Germans and the Arabs, the blond men from Thule and the men from the desert, have one thing in common. They hate Jews.'

Marshal Foch coaxed the lantern into life again. His mood had changed. He touched my shoulder and pushed me forward slightly.

'Now I will show you a most interesting and unusual sight,' he said to me. I tripped and my foot dragged on a corner of the sacking which covered the floor to reveal the figure of a dead bullock on its side with its tongue outstretched.

'What is this?'

'It is the story, as I told you. Proserpine's mother goes to Jupiter to ask for her. Please come.'

'No. I want to see everything.'

'We cannot stay here long,' said the Marshal impatiently. 'This picture shows the famine Ceres inflicted on mankind when she learned that her daughter had been stolen. Eventually Pluto had to hand the girl over. It was blackmail. She wasn't a virgin any more of course, but that didn't bother the gods. The house of immorality, remember. What are you doing?'

I kicked off the rest of the sacking. Now I recalled the story. A mosaic on the other side of the floor showed Venus leading the young girl out of her hiding-place through a meadow of flowers. In the background mount Etna was in eruption. Marshal Foch said, 'I think the artist had a sense of humour. She wants Pluto to rape the girl. Why? Because then Venus will govern the spirits of the dead as well.'

We came to the last mosaic. I took the lantern from the other man. Proserpine and Pluto were shown as man and wife. In the palm of her hand lay seven seeds. I remembered it all now: Jupiter released Ceres' daughter provided she had not tasted food during her stay in Hell. But she had eaten seven seeds of the pomegranate. So she can only spend part of the year in the sunlight and when she is down with her husband Ceres makes sure nothing grows. It is of course, I thought, a myth of how the seasons come about. I noticed Pluto had put his arm around his wife and was clasping her towards him. Was her head inclined ever so slightly towards his?

Marshal Foch took back the lantern and we went through an opening into a little room. Along one side was a shelf with an alcove above it and he pointed at a painting on the wall.

'This was one of the bedrooms. Look!'

At first all I could see was a pair of buttocks, the flesh tones hard to distinguish from the brown clay of the wall. I realised we were watching a couple in the act of fucking. The woman had dark hair piled on top of her head. She looked nothing like Barbara. One arm was raised and she was pressing the face of a bearded man against her neck. She was naked except for a gold bangle on each arm. The man was holding one of her legs high up against his belly so that her buttocks were parted. His other arm had snaked around her and he was pressing her closely into him. Her body was almost lifted off the ground as she grasped his black penis with her other hand and pushed it into her vagina.

Marshal Foch's chuckle turned into a dry cough and he said again with the tone of a magician showing off his best trick: 'Why shouldn't there be love in Hell?'

6.   Madame Foch

I did not respond. After a moment's silence the Marshal left the bedroom and the two of us climbed back up the stairs. Locking the trapdoor, he spread leaves over it and strode downhill towards the back of the museum. I followed him into a small room shuttered against the light. Marshal Foch opened a cupboard and brought out a bottle of arak and two glasses. Pieces of maps lay on the floor around a desk.

'The Germans took all the maps,' he said as he poured the colourless liquor into the tumblers. 'They needed fuel and maps. They didn't even know where they were. Have a drink. I have a favour to ask.'

He pushed the glass across the desk.

'I told you life has become difficult here. Things have changed with the killing of Yusuf. The Germans showed people what can be done when they shot him. They gave guns to some of the young men. Nobody will harm me. I am a Frenchman. I have lived here for twenty years. But I have a wife.'

Marshal Foch touched his fingertips together as though holding a small invisible head between them before going on.

'Can you take her to Tabarka when you leave, with a letter to a friend of mine?'

So I talked to the driver and it cost the Marshal two bottles of arak to arrange the journey. The trucks were ready by the side of the road that afternoon when he appeared wearing an official cap that made him look more than ever like a First World War general. Behind him stood Madame Foch, a silent figure taller than her husband, carrying a brown parcel and shrouded from head to foot in a black cloak. I was helping her into the back of the truck when I caught sight of Barbara's sunburned face staring from the other truck with her lips curled back in disgust and I had to silence savagely the moanings of my fellow-patients who were asking, 'Why have we got to carry a wog?'

As the vehicles moved off the old general bowed slowly and deeply. Replacing his kepi he stood at ease with hands behind his back and legs slightly apart, a small figure becoming even smaller in the distance. The vehicle bounced along the highway and I sat next to Madame Foch without touching any part of her. I reached inside my pocket and brought out her husband's gift. It was the figurine of a woman made of baked clay, about four inches long. One side of her face was damaged but the other showed a young girl with a pointed chin and laughing mouth. I turned it this way and that, comparing the damaged side with the perfect one.

Just at that moment the truck came to a halt in the middle of the road. The guard jumped out but came back a minute later and lit a cigarette, saying 'Lad in front's got a puncture.' He was putting his rifle back inside the tailgate when things began to happen very fast. The soldier coughed heavily as though the smoke had gone down the wrong way and he slid down the tailgate and disappeared. An insect buzzed by my ear and holes appeared in the tarpaulin covering opposite. I dropped to the floor and crawled towards the back of the truck. As I clambered over the tailgate and trod on the soldier I heard more shots. He grunted but didn't move and I crawled under the truck. The firing stopped and two soldiers dragged a heavy sack across the road towards where I lay. When they dropped the sack I saw it was a young man. The boy wriggled around but a boot kicked him in the side and he kept still. He wore grey German battledress and had rope sandals on his feet. Something was wrong with one of his arms where the tunic was torn.

I lay on the road under the truck and watched the boy reach into the pocket of his trousers with his other hand and pull out a big stick grenade. He couldn't get the damaged arm over to unscrew the fuse so he rocked to and fro until the arm flopped over next to the grenade. Suddenly the boy's head exploded with a bang and fragments of his skull hit me in the face. With my sleeve I wiped my eyes clear and saw that the grenade had rolled towards my legs. Very carefully and slowly I picked it up and looked at it. A lot of people were shouting.

7.   Bella's diary

Tabarka Hospital. April 1st.

I have just finished a letter to Papa which Philippe is taking. He is visiting his brother and says he will look for Papa at the museum. He won't go near the town after I told him about the ambush by Moussef and his gang. I didn't tell Papa the whole story because I don't want to worry him, but I said they put nails on the road to stop the lorries. Weren't they awful? The British soldier who was shot died on the way to the hospital. But I didn't tell Papa about that either.

The other soldiers were terribly nervous after they killed Moussef. When captain Dodo climbed out from under the truck they nearly shot him as well. He had a grenade and he dropped it or they would have killed him. I screamed because he was covered with blood and I thought he had been injured. I ran to him, I was so worried, but it wasn't his blood, it was Moussef's!

After they fixed the puncture, the soldiers crawled all over the road on their hands and knees looking for more nails. Captain Dodo and I sat in the front and I had to point out where I thought there might be more ambushes. All the time the wounded man was moaning and shouting. They didn't have any morphine, the captain said. When it got dark we stopped and camped in the woods. Captain Dodo found a blanket and looked after me. I told him I wasn't Papa's wife at all but his daughter and he went quiet for a moment and then he just laughed. In the morning when he was bringing some tea one of the nurses spat in my face and slapped captain Dodo as hard as she could across the cheek. He didn't laugh at that. But I don't know what the woman was so upset about.

I had to warn Papa about the bad news that uncle Joseph isn't here any more. He has gone to Algiers. He said that the only reason the Arabs aren't killing our people in Tabarka is because the English and Americans are here. Or he might go to Palestine if he can get on a boat. He sold the

29

shop so I didn't have any job or anywhere to live. I was scared for a while but something wonderful happened today. Captain Dodo is so kind. He has found me work up here at the hospital with the English cleaning the wards. He came to see me at Joseph's shop in the corner of the main square. It was shut up and he knocked on the glass door. I kept the door open all the time we talked because I knew the neighbours would report me if I took a man inside.

'The shop has been sold,' I said, 'and tomorrow I have to move out.'

It wasn't entirely true because the buyer's wife has offered to let me stay as a servant but it had the effect on him that I was hoping for.

He told me to pack my things and waited under the plane trees. I watched from behind the curtain as the shopkeepers leaned against the shop doors or sat on cane-backed chairs and called for tea. Abdullah the tea boy ran across the street and sold Dodo a cup of sweet tea in a glass. I bet he charged him five times the usual price. When I locked the shop and gave the key to the baker he gravely presented me with a fresh baguette. Holding the bread in one hand and my bag in the other, I walked quickly to the jeep and climbed in, arranging the folds of the cloak around my head. I could feel the eyes of the little crowd follow the jeep around the square as I let the air blow the cloak away from my face. I knew exactly the dirty talk they were having when I saw Alphonse the tobacconist, who is from Marseilles, turn and say something to his wife who had come from the storeroom. I bet it was a remark like, 'Joseph's niece has gone away with the English captain. Paul gave her a baguette as a leaving present.' His wife spat past him onto the pavement and I could imagine her replying that now there were two baguettes in the jeep.

I threw the bread into the gutter when we had turned the corner.

April 3rd.

The military hospital is perched on a hill above the Mediterranean. It is an old French sanatorium and has a funny tarry smell. Ahmed the gatekeeper says it is the scent of creosote from the masks the patients wore to try to kill the tuberculosis bacilli. Broad verandas shade the rooms from the heat and the place is surrounded by a large dusty garden. Ahmed says the matron has named the wards after historic British victories. She is a Scotswoman who ran away from home in the last war to serve as a volunteer nurse, he says, and married a surgeon who died of flu at the end of the war – he got on his motorbike in Glasgow perfectly well and when he reached Edinburgh he took to his bed and died in a few hours. How Ahmed knows all this I have no idea! Matron Hamilton is a striking woman with iron grey hair gathered in a bun and a large figure that is well set off by the blue and red of the Queen Alexandra's uniform. She has put me to work on Jutland ward as a maid to start with and promises I can move to nursing auxiliary if I do well.

Jutland has big windows with high ceilings and metal fans that turn slowly. I am up before dawn and have to make the ward spotless before the inspection each morning. I empty the patients' ash trays and use Dettol to wash their bedpans and specimen bottles in the sluice next to the kitchen. Then I pull out the metal bedsteads from the walls and crawl underneath to scrub the floor clean with carbolic soap until each bed stands neatly with its castors all facing inwards over its own reflection on the polished floor. The metal lids of the hot oil baths that are used to sterilise hypodermic syringes have to be cleaned until they shine and when I lift them off the stink of the oil inside make me think I am in the engine room of some vast hospital ship, even though I have never even sailed across to France.

April 10th.

I am remembering all the English I learned at school and now I help the nurses make the beds. The ward sister's inspection is the big moment of the morning shift and the nurses grow agitated as the time draws near, hissing across the bed, 'Turn down the blankets first and loosen the sheets. Now, roll the patient over to me. Put your arm through his, so, and heave him up from the bed. Shake out the pillow. Make sure the open end is away from the door. The open end, I said, you stupid Arab. Sister likes everything neat and tidy.'

After the sister has gone I fetch the breakfast trolley on its rubber tyres and set out the tin containers of salted bacon or sausages with doorstep-sized slabs of bread and margarine on the table in the middle of the ward. The men who can get up shuffle over in flapping dressing gowns and oakum slippers. I lift the big enamelled teapot with both hands and pour from its long spout the brown sweet tea. Poticare, the senior doctor, a fair balding man with a squint, has his eyes on me and I have to be careful to straighten up quickly if he appears in the wards or I feel his hand caressing me from behind.

8.   Jutland

I spent a lot of time on Jutland Ward with Bella after I found her a job, though I was in a different, convalescent section of the old hospital. When the nurses weren't nearby I would stand and talk slowly to Bella about my past life, about how I had wanted to be a doctor as a boy, about my prowess on the sports field and going to India just before the war.

'Life in India is so much fun,' I told her. 'I stayed one time with the Nizam of Hyderabad and he gave me a bedroom as large as Jutland Ward. I played polo and made a century against the Nizam's private cricket team.'

I spoke of coming to Africa, about Cairo and the crowded streets and the city of the dead where people picnicked in the tombs and the pyramids at Giza. I described to her what it was like to live in the desert with its vast distances and its silence and the cold of the nights but I did not tell her anything about the war because I did not know what to say.

I remember her as though it was yesterday. She was a tall young woman of nineteen years with a firm neck that supported a big head with a jutting chin and a large nose ending in a sharp point above her full curved lips.Her complexion was pale with a tint of olive and she was careful to keep out of the sunlight. Over her broad shoulders flowed a mass of thick dark-red hair the colour of chestnuts in autumn when they have fallen from the trees. She told me later that she tied her hair into braids after washing so that when she shook out her long tresses they were slightly crinkly and gave off different highlights of colour from light red to deep auburn. She was proud of this but she believed that her finest feature was not her hair nor even her complexion - though she loved the fact that she was as white as any other European woman. She was proudest of her huge eyes with their green-speckled irises, and above all of the whites of her eyes that went right round the iris, so that she could look at a man and make him feel that he alone was the centre of her world. Looking back I suppose Bella's gaze was slightly pop-eyed but it dazzled the young doctors and patients. In the mornings, she said, she would always spend a few minutes rubbing a little kohl into her eyes as she crouched in front of the looking-glass before going to work in the wards.

For most of the day I sat by the bedside of my friend Douglas Carr, a tank commander who had been wounded at Mareth, and tried to get him to talk or play cards or even listen as I read out the daily news. Douglas and our friend Jonny had arrived with me at the hospital on the same day, rattling up the bad road along the coast. But Jonny had died and I feared that Douglas Carr was going the same way with his terrible sweating, high temperature and convulsions from the septic wound in his arm that refused to heal. Jutland was full of patients like Douglas Carr and there was nothing to be done. Morphine to kill pain was the commonest medication.

After breakfast I watched the nurses go from bed to bed. The hospital was a noisy place. The white enamel dressings trolley jingled and glittered as the nurses pushed it along. Metal bowls, tins of dressings and bottles of coloured lotion chinked against each other. The glass ampoules of morphine lay next to the syringes. They worked in pairs. One nurse rolled the patient over, exposed his buttocks and dabbed on spirit. The other broke the ampoule's seal and filled the hypo, holding it to the light and letting the bubble of morphine run up to the top of the needle, then pinching the skin and pushing the plunger home. As they ladled out medication and took temperatures with their mercury thermometers, the smell of drugs mingled with Bella's floor polish.

Evening prayers ended the working day. The night shift came on duty, carrying their billycans of food and yawning. The day nurses briefed them and glanced at their fob watches with the habitual anxious look of hospital staff who are always a little behind time. They watched with folded hands as the night sister stood in the middle of the ward and fished a small prayer book out of her pocket. I stood in the shadows and waited for Bella to finish. The lamp made a ladder of light on the polished floor towards the old French crucifix above the entrance as she began the prayer, 'Lighten our darkness we beseech thee, O Lord...'

I never talked to Bella of my growing love for her. I hovered around the subject with my quiet slow talk like a small bird flitting about the feeding tray in a garden who is afraid to land in case the cat jumps up and catches her But I saw that Bella became more aware how clever and attractive she was. She quickly picked up enough English to understand what the doctors wanted, and she set out to charm them. It helped that after a few weeks she was allowed to dress as though she was a real nurse in a light blue shirt with denim slacks cut tight at the waist. Above her waist her breasts pushed out the pockets of the shirt and as her tall figure strode down the corridors or bent over a patient I noticed how tightly she had pinned up her hair to show the pale olive skin at the back of her neck. I thought she was a goddess.

9.   Bella's diary

April 28th.

This morning as I was walking towards Jutland I saw an olive-green Humber car draw up at the main entrance. The driver was a military policeman with a moustache and brick red complexion. A small man who wore red tabs on his shoulders was next to emerge. He stood wiping his forehead with a handkerchief. The third visitor was a civilian, a man of medium height in his mid-forties with a thick mop of black hair parted near the crown. His face was pale like he was ill and he was dressed in a dark suit with no consideration for the weather. He carried a small box carefully in both hands as he walked up the steps to the veranda where in peacetime the tuberculosis patients sat in the shade.

The man with red tabs turned in a fussy manner to the military policeman and snapped out, 'Sergeant, you really ought to be in charge of Professor Florey's package.'

The sergeant's face reminds me of the local policeman in our town. It has an expressionless and detached quality so that you feel you are looking at a profile even when seeing him from the front. He took the box and marched off with the matron.

The civilian's sharp eyes darted around as I walked by. I could tell what he was noting: the tired expression of a passing nurse, the walls smeared with grime by the passage of many bodies and the sluggish movement of the fans overhead that signalled an unreliable electrical current. Poticare offered tea but the civilian waved the idea aside.

'Perhaps later. We mustn't shuffle our feet. The drug isn't stable when it's hot as blazes like this. Where shall we start?'

Poticare grabbed his clipboard tightly.

'Let's begin with Carr in Jutland.'

I ran ahead of them and watched them enter the ward from my place by the kitchen. Dodo's friend in the corner was dying, I knew that much even without the evil omen of the red screens. His heart was giving out. The ward sister came from behind the screens pushing Dodo in front of her. He disappeared into the corridor and she looked around for a nurse before beckoning me over. 'Run to the dispensary,' she said, 'and get the sergeant to bring the professor's box.' When we came back the sister took the box as carefully as though it was an unexploded bomb and the soldier sat down at the long table to wait. He drank tea but he wouldn't talk. His Browning pistol stayed holstered at his side.

I watched the professor unlock the box and lift out a small glass ampoule with a yellow liquid inside. Poticare pushed the hypo needle through the rubber seal, filled it, and began to depress the plunger until the liquid bled at the top of the needle. With a sharp intake of breath the brigadier stopped him. 'Don't waste even a drop. The drug costs three thousand dollars per ounce. Give me back the ampoule.' Poticare pinched the feverish man's flesh and injected the medicine that was far more valuable than gold. When they had all gone I copied down his medical notes. They say: Patient has temperature of 102 degrees F and rapid fluctuating heartbeat. Injected 2.5 cc of Professor Florey's drug by drip.

Monday, May 3rd
Douglas Carr has bled heavily from his right arm and collapsed. The sister gave him 2 pints of blood. Dodo is frantic.

May 4th
Dosage has been increased to 4 cc daily.

May 5th
Dosage is at 6 cc daily. Dodo and I believe he is dying.

May 6th

We are nearly at the end. Douglas is bleeding again and his temperature has shot up to 103 degrees F. They took him to the operating theatre, opened and cleaned out the wound and put in the drug in powder form before sewing him up. Poticare is injecting 3 cc every 3 hours. I don't think he will last the night.

May 7th.
This is a miracle. Douglas's temperature is back to normal. His pulse is strong and the sister says he is getting better.

May 10th.
Dosage reduced to 3 cc every 6 hours.

May 13th.
Dosage ended. Douglas is up and running about. Not just walking, but running. He is chasing us around the big table at Jutland. Sometimes he jumps over it. The girls fall on the floor laughing when he catches us and even the sister can't be harsh with him. There is a festival atmosphere in the hospital. In each ward soldiers whom the doctors wrote off have recovered completely after a few days on the new drug. The diseases we never talk about with men (I mean sexual diseases) respond particularly well. The sister says it is the best fighting soldiers who love the risk of visiting the local whores. The madams give the women small doses of sulpha drugs bought on the black market. They mask the disease, she says, so when the women are inspected they appear to be clean, but it is not enough to stop them passing it on from one soldier to the next. The fastest recoveries are the men who have gone down with the clap. It doesn't seem fair to me.

May 15th.

Last night Poticare invited me over to the doctor's mess to have supper and listen to Professor Florey talk about how he developed his wonder drug. I still won't let him do what he wants to me though. The professor looked tired but he told a wonderful story about his white mice over corned beef, tinned peas and mashed potatoes in the old monks' refectory. I will try to remember it all.

'It was the time of that gorgeous Dunkirk weather. D'you remember?' He speaks with what Dodo says is an Australian accent.

'The blossoms were all out on the trees when I walked through the parks to the lab. Brilliant skies, sunlight and a sense of everything falling apart through the air. We had been working on mice for months. The trick was to infect them with the bug for blood poisoning so they would die in 24 to 36 hours. First we injected eight mice and put them into two cages side by side, four mice in each cage and crumbled some biscuits to see how they would feed. The lab boys put labels up. The first four mice they called Alex, Bertie, Charlie and Dick, and the second unlucky four, the control group who wouldn't get any drug, they named Goering, Goebbels, Himmler and Hitler.

An hour later we gave the lucky mice their shots. Charlie and Dick got more penicillin every two hours. It was Saturday morning. We took it in turns to watch them all night. The mice which hadn't been given any drug started staggering around soon after midnight and by morning all the four unlucky rodents had turned up their paws. The others were all right. The staphylococcus hadn't killed them.'

A doctor sitting next to me banged his fist down so the mugs and tin plates jumped.

'Curtains for Hitler and his mates!' he laughed.

'That was when we knew we had something really extraordinary on our hands. But even a year ago,' Florey continued, 'we hadn't a hope of making enough to use on more than a few patients. And now Cairns and I are touring the Middle East trying it out in the best hospitals. Hopefully you'll have more than enough for your needs by the autumn. Thanks to the Yanks.'

Poticare leaned forward. His face was flushed with excitement and two glasses of gin. I had had to fight him off all through the meal.

'I don't understand, professor. What have our American allies got to do with penicillin?'

Florey explained. Apparently the Americans have the laboratories ready to go as well as the facilities to freeze dry the penicillin once it has been made. 'The professor did post-grad work with the research head of Pfizer before the war,' added the brigadier.

After the meal I was drinking tea with a young doctor when Florey passed by.

'Is there any chance of being able to use your drug on the local people here, Professor?' the doctor asked. 'The hospital in the town is in a bad way. Not enough medicines and the Germans took all the sulphonamides away with them.'

The sweating little brigadier overheard and came across wagging a finger. 'Penicillin is for Forces personnel only,' he said in his fussy way. 'We can sort out the locals when we've won the war.'

I suppose Papa and I are classified as locals too.

10.   The movie show

I will never forget the time Bella and I made love – the only time. It was just after Florey left for England. I wasn't allowed into Jutland to see Douglas but she came to the door of the ward and told me about my friend's progress, how at first the news was poor and then dreadful, and then became quickly, astonishingly good. I spent the day walking up and down the corridor outside, trying to correct the limp in my leg. Bella could see me passing as she worked and sometimes I stopped and looked for her, and if the nurses were not around she would come up to me and we would hold hands quietly, looking at the red screens. I felt that the miracle we were witnessing had somehow bound us together.

She began to talk about her strange childhood in that isolated town beyond the hills. She went to school there and by the time she was sixteen only two other girls were left in the class. The school closed when France fell to the Germans, she said, and the teachers ran away. She wore European clothes to school: a long cotton dress and brown boots but walked to and from the schoolhouse in her cloak. The Arab girls avoided the boys after school but because she was a Frenchwoman, she considered it appropriate to behave as an equal of the males and she talked with them and let them walk her to the bottom of the street where she lived. But she never allowed any of them to touch her. I was the first.

On this particular day a cinema crew arrived at the hospital and the patients and nurses came to the chapel to watch the film. Bella helped the soldiers string up the screen in front of the altar. As the swing music from the speakers played she whirled across the floor. She told me she had always gone to the films in the main square when travelling shows came to the town. She loved watching Charlie Chaplin with his funny moustache and the France she had never seen with its vineyards and cities. But in the town, she said, they only had silent films projected onto the whitewashed walls of the mairie. She came and sat beside me and I could feel her warm flesh pressed against my side. Across the room the projectionist doused the lights. The newsreel began with martial music and showed Roosevelt and Churchill at Casablanca. Bella pointed at de Gaulle and nudged me.

When the footage of battles came on I knew which bits were faked. I watched Tommies run up to a barbed wire entanglement and fling themselves forward to flatten it with their bodies so that a pistol-waving officer could jump over.

'Ouch!' shouted a voice. I looked along the benches. Several patients were jerking their heads away. Civilians appeared on the screen, Arabs. Small children held the hands of their older siblings as they walked and mothers carried babies. They had scarves or veils covering their faces. A cart drawn by a donkey was piled high with simple household items - blankets, a table, a metal basin. The scene changed and now young men in European suits stood in a city street. They waved at the camera and ripped off the yellow stars from their coat pockets and threw them into the dirt. A scared little boy in shorts looked up as a uniformed doctor jabbed a needle into his forearm. Bella turned her face to me.

'What were the Arabs doing?'

'Running away from the fighting, I suppose.'

'But where were they going to?'

Before I could think of an answer the scene moved to long columns of surrendering troops and a British and an American voice started a dialogue. The American was called Joe and the Englishman was George.

'George, I've got an idea! Why don't we stay together after the war - the same gang as now? What couldn't we do?'

'You mean build more houses than ever was built before, and ships, thousands of ships?'

'Yeah George. And nobody would be hungry any more. Instead of blowing things up we'd build dams in the desert and roads through the jungle, and who knows maybe bridges across all the seas. Bring the smiles back to kids' faces!'

'Yessir Joe! And knock the block off anybody who wants to start another war.'

The film ended with aeroplanes flying overhead and a waving of Allied flags. 'After Africa, on to Europe!' cried George and the lights came on. I stretched out my bad leg. Bella's nails were digging into my arm. She tugged at me and I got up and followed her out of the chapel. A few sniggers went with us.

At first I couldn't find her. She called my name and I turned towards her, thinking she had never looked lovelier as she stood adjusting the kerchief around her head, with her shadow lying behind her on the path in the moonlight. She took my arm.

'Let's walk down to the beach.'

As we crossed the road her smell and the scent of roses she used electrified me with the possibility of making love. The path led past bushes of oleander and crossed a stretch of dunes that separated the beach from the groves of olives and lemon trees. To the left lay the river with the bridges and beyond it the town. I would often go to the beach before Bella arrived and hunt among the objects thrown up on the shore. I found driftwood, mostly palms or pieces of olive wood, and sometimes oak logs that had been carried down from the mountains. Once after a storm I found an empty liferaft.

The wind blew hard along the beach, a hot wind that scooped up the sand and threw it against our bodies as soon as we crossed the dunes. It stung our exposed skin and we moved closer together as we walked to the deserted lighthouse on the point. Where there was most shelter we sat down with our backs against the curved wall and I kissed her. She pushed her tongue into my open mouth and touched the wet top of my mouth with its fluttering tip. I stroked that lovely taut skin at the base of her neck and she slid slowly down the wall until she was lying with me half on top of her. We carried on kissing and I began to unbutton her shirt with my other hand. I found a nipple and began to stroke it gently with a round motion as it stiffened and grew larger. She moved so she could straighten her legs and rubbed her left knee between my legs and then she felt the hardness of my prick. My hand moved from her naked breast down to between her thighs and I began to stroke her but she pushed it away.

I had a bit of sexual experience. In England I had kissed a girl and in India I lost my virginity to a whore. Her father had been a sergeant in a Norfolk regiment and her mother had also been a whore. In a small room with a door but no window she removed my clothes, stripped down to her knickers and rubbed my body with jasmine oil. Then she knelt over me and rubbed my prick until I came over her breasts. On my second visit she took her knickers off and the last time she put my prick inside her but pulled it out before I came. I was still very young and thought I was developing a relationship with her.

In Cairo I went with a few friends to the house of Kore. It had a blue and white door in an alley that ran behind the Greek church. Scuffy said the girls were mainly Greeks not Arabs and clean as these places went. A small boy in a thobe jumped up and banged on the door when he saw us coming, and Scuffy gave him a penny. The others went upstairs but I stayed at the bar. A French kiss in the Home Counties and several visits to a brothel did not prepare me for Barbara when she took me to the nurses' lavatory on a sticky afternoon, and afterwards she was angry at what she called in her squeaky voice 'your gaucheness.' But nothing in the world could ever compare to Bella and the love she showed to me that evening.

She began to tug on my prick and in a while she pulled her body out from under mine. Her breasts brushed against my shirt as she knelt over me and took me in her mouth. When I started to jerk and moan she pulled away and rubbed the prick against her breasts until I came over her nipples. In the moonlight that was made stronger by the reflection from the sea my semen lying on her skin looked like spilled milk. For a while we cuddled on the hard concrete plinth of the lighthouse. I put my arm around Bella's head and she wiped her breasts with her kerchief.

'I love you,' I said.

'Darling, I love you too. I want us always to be together.'

She stroked my hair as I confessed how much I cared for her. She put a finger gently to my lips to quiet me.

An idea came into my head: 'If you were an auxiliary nurse you could go with the hospital when it moves. Otherwise you'll have to stay behind in Africa and when will I ever see you again?' Bella ran her finger around the little indentation on my temple.

'Oh darling that would be wonderful! I am a Frenchwoman after all and the English and the French are allies.'

So I left my signet ring and a five pound note with the hospital clerk the next morning and got Bella Imago, a French citizen, added to the roll of auxiliary nurses. And that was the only time we made love. Three days later I was examined by a red-faced Scottish doctor who pronounced me fit for active service despite the limp.

'Only we can't have you back in the infantry, laddy,' he said. 'Too much marching will do that leg again. You'll be flying in, like a bloody VIP.'

I kissed her passionately when I was ordered to Algeria for training in gliders and the time came to say good-bye but we had no second chance to go down to the beach. We wondered whether we would ever see each other again, and we very nearly didn't.

11.   Bella's diary

May 18th.

Last night I finally did it. I had been thinking about it for some time because I knew he would be going soon. But the film show made me understand that the British are planning to leave us all behind with the Arabs while they go off to Europe. They want to abandon me, a young woman with my life still to live! And the British have so much power. Haven't I watched men who would have perished from disease as Mama did get up and walk after being given the penicillin? Afterwards I was so angry I had to run outside and be sick. As I wiped the sick away from my mouth I decided to take the matter into my own hands. I found the courage to seduce Dodo.

I took him out as I had planned to the lighthouse on the beach and did with him what Moussef and I used to do. A strange idea popped into my mind as I was licking his prick: He's just like Moussef, I thought. He tastes just the same. Why did I imagine each man would taste different?

Now he has gone to the hospital office to see about getting me a promotion and I am sitting here remembering the first time with Moussef. It was the day after the archaeologists and the schoolteachers went back to Paris and left Papa on his own. That morning the students could not get into the building and I stood to one side and listened to the boys.

Ali chattered away as usual: 'All the French ships have been sunk by the English and the Germans are in Paris.'

Moussef jumped down from where he had been sitting on the stone wall and laughed. 'Soon they will come here as well and free us from the French,' he said. I was silent.

After a while the group dispersed and I moved to Moussef's side as we walked home. He was tall and funny and kind. At the corner of my street I suggested we visit Papa at the museum. The sun beat down and

46

we drew our cloaks over our heads. Near the site of the villa where the archaeologists had been working, I turned to him.

'I am French,' I said. 'You don't want to drive me away, do you? I think you like me.'

The darkness as he followed me down the stairs into the villa blinded us both. I was trembling and I let him lift up my dress. But I knew that I must keep my legs closed and I used my mouth. I had read in a magazine from Paris that this was what French ladies did when they didn't want to have a baby. I closed my lips around the base of Moussef's prick and licked him with my tongue. He tasted salty for a few moments and then he ejaculated into my mouth and I pulled spluttering away. I know when to pull away in good time now! Neither of us said anything as we walked on to the museum. He promised that I would never be harmed as long as he was alive. So matters went until the night the Germans came.

Papa always believed the peasants would see the Nazis as a way to get rid of outsiders. Enemy columns would come across the mountains looking for petrol and diesel. It was a war for oil, Papa said, that was obvious from the start. I never expected it to come to our own town though. But who does?

Now in an instant down at the lighthouse, when I tasted Dodo, I relived the events of that cold night when I saw Moussef for the last time. We were in Yusuf's kitchen when we saw the German trucks stop by the whitewashed wall of the mayor's offices. Past the war memorial the soldiers marched towards the shop led by a tall man in a cloak and hood. The glass door showed them the lighted kitchen with the four of us sitting around a table.

'Open! Open the door!' the sergeant shouted.

Yusuf stood up and his wine glass rolled sideways into Papa's lap. The sergeant brought Ariel and Papa and me into the street with the old man. The tall informer pointed at the boy and the officer nodded.

'Keep him too. Sergeant Meyer, let the others go.'

I knew at once that it was Moussef who was betraying us and shouted curses but Papa pulled me away. The officer was only interested in questioning Yusuf.

'Where you are hiding the fuel?'

'I swear I have given you everything.'

'They are Jews,' added Moussef.

The sergeant came out of the shop carrying a helmet and rifle.

'My old equipment from the last war,' said Yusuf

'The Jews' garage is round this corner.'

The soldiers searched inside while Yusuf and the boy stood in shirtsleeves against the garage wall. A crowd gathered in the alleyway and Papa wanted to leave but I made him stay. The soldiers rolled out an oildrum while we were arguing.

'Cooking oil,' said Ariel without conviction in his voice, but the sergeant was already reading the label out loud. It was diesel fuel.

'Yehudi, yehudi!' chanted the crowd around us, repeating what Moussef said. The Arabs grasped instinctively what was going to happen. I thought perhaps I could rescue them – I don't know what I thought.

'Take the diesel fuel to the trucks and set fire to this building,' ordered the officer. The crowd followed noisily back into the square. Oildrums were loaded onto the trucks. Ariel and Yusuf waited meekly by the war memorial with its statue. The crowd formed a circle around them. Papa kept trying to pull me away.

'I'll put the two Jews in the truck, shall I sir?' said the sergeant in a gentle insinuating voice.

'No, Meyer,' the officer replied. 'I will take care of this. You two. You two. Kneel down.'

The officer turned the old helmet in his hands for a moment. I have often wondered what he was thinking. Perhaps he was remembering his own Papa who never came back. The helmet fell to the ground and he shot them both with his pistol in front of us all. The trucks drove away and the bodies were left by the memorial. Some in the crowd looted the shop while others were round the corner putting out the fire.

After that I stayed indoors like an Arab woman and never saw him alive again. Only I saw his body when it lay next to Dodo's truck. Moussef did try to keep his side of our bargain, I realise now. He died trying to protect me.

12. Mascara

Peter and Lawrence were the best friends I ever had, and I met them in the last few weeks of my life. Peter and I became acquainted first in a bar in Algeria. He was only really happy in a bar or in the air. We had been drinking for some hours together and I don't remember everything we talked about. But I remember the way the barman looked at Peter when he banged on the makeshift surface of the bar with his tumbler.

'Barman, another glass of brandy.'

The barman closed his eyes and poured out a measure of banana extract and industrial alcohol. He was a lithe man with Brylcreemed hair and an immaculate mess jacket. I pondered once again on how it was that the further you got away from the front line, the better the quality of the troops. The barman was glowing with health. He was so authentically a barman that he could have taken the part in Hollywood, serving Bogart a drink in 'Casablanca'. Where on earth had he got the Brylcreem from?

'Two hours.' Peter continued, the blood trickling down his chin from where he had cut his lip on the tumbler, 'two hours. One hundred and twenty minutes. In terms of seconds, that's seven thousand and ...'

He banged the glass on the surface of the bar.

'Barman, I want another drink.'

Peter looked terrible. His Wing Commander's jacket was smeared with grease and banana liquor and his little blue eyes were bloodshot.

'...Seven thousand one hundred and twenty seconds,' he said with triumph, running his finger delicately round the rim of his glass. 'That's all the flying your typical glider pilot has done.' He carried on with his story.

'It wa a hush-hush operation, old man. Wind against us all the way. Intercom failed. The local resistance were supposed to set up a radio beacon to guide us in but there was no signal and we were running low on fuel. So I had to abort the op. Ran into cloud on the home run and I climbed for height. Flaps started to ice up and she flew heavy so I started moving them up and down to clear the ice off. That slowed us down more. Then the glider began to bugger around behind us. Her towrope was icing up and her weight was pulling us down as well. So there we were, somewhere in the mountains, in cloud, no visibility, losing height, running low on fuel.'

'What happened next?' I asked, trying to drink the alcohol without breathing its fumes.

'Plane kicked upwards. The towrope had gone. Either it had broken or Strathdee dropped it because he knew we were all finished if he didn't. Plane kicked upwards, we gained height and got home with a thimbleful of fuel to spare.'

He wiped the red and yellow mixture off his chin and licked his finger. I waited.

'Strathdee crashed onto the side of a mountain. Half the lads didn't make it. The rest tried to get to Sweden but they were rounded up by the Jerries and shot. It was a hush-hush operation. You could have used Strathdee here. He had more hours flying gliders than any half-dozen of these kids.'

Peter's elbow slipped on some spillage. I caught up my new friend and steered him out of the mess bar across the courtyard of the little hotel while he repeated, 'Mayday, Mayday.' Peter had a room with a high ceiling, a beautiful tiled floor and long windows. I dropped him onto his camp bed and arranged the mosquito netting. He was still talking about 'wooden aircraft' and 'flying coffins' when I closed the door and made my way upstairs. I booted a few of the giant local cockroaches out of the room and sprinkled flea-powder across the doorway and around the skirting as a barrier to entry before I went to bed.

During the night I woke once to a curious rustling sound like a silk dress. At daybreak I was moving towards the window when I stopped and looked down. The floor of the room was coated like the bottom of an ocean with the carapaces of dead cockroaches that had been dismembered and eaten. The survivors had been shut in by my barrier of flea-powder and were stumbling around on their thousandth circuit, like a column of the foreign legion abandoned in the middle of the desert. On the soles of my bare feet was stuck the purple residue of crushed bodies. For a moment I stood frozen, unable to move and revolted by the thought of treading on the insects and then I improvised a shovel and emptied the lot, dead, dying and alive, out of the window. From the courtyard below came shouts of rage. Looking down I saw the wogs getting up from where they had been sipping tea and shaking bits of cockroaches off their clothes.

I laughed out of sheer joy at the morning and gazed at the sunlit landscape. The town stood on a double hill split by a gorge, and other hills around had gardens of vines and olive trees and were topped by windmills. Beyond the land fell away to a wide brown plain of dusty fields, the occasional clump of olive trees and scrubland. In the distance were airstrips with their temporary buildings, aircraft and crates. The plain was bare with no walls and few trees: good country for landing gliders, I guessed.

After breakfast we drove down the winding dirt track to the airstrip. It was about 2,000 yards long and had been scraped through wheatfields that looked as thin as poor grass in seed. The engine oil that had been spread over the surface to compact it was already cracking and the dust formed little twisters in the wind. Dozens of aircraft and gliders lay scattered as though a giant boy had been playing with them and had gone for lunch. Peter weaved at speed along the strip, sometimes under the wings of the planes.

'C-47s, Dakotas, Yank kites,' he said, waving one hand and lighting a cigarette with the other. 'I've heard they don't have self-sealing petrol tanks. One bullet hole and all the fuel, what the Yanks call gas, pours out. Scary.'

We narrowly missed a Dakota's tailwheel.

'I'll show you my Albemarle,' he said. We got out of the jeep next to a large aircraft with two engines and Peter kicked a tyre.

'I'm taking this crate back to Blighty tomorrow to fetch some more gliders. Dear old Albemarle. She's too slow to evade Jerry fighters, hasn't got enough guns to shoot them down, and her bomb bay is too small. Perfect for towing gliders though. As for the Horsa,' he laughed, 'well, you'll soon learn all about the Horsa. It's the most wooden aircraft ever built.'

But Peter couldn't find the Horsa. Finally a big black man with an American accent directed us to a corner of the airstrip. As we drew near I could see the pile of wooden crates. A sergeant wearing the wings of a glider pilot saluted smartly. Charlie Coombs was over six feet tall with wavy auburn hair and a splendid moustache.

'Just taking it out of the boxes, sir,' he barked out. 'We've rounded up a load of wogs to help.'

The sergeant knew his job. He chalked an outline of the glider on the ground so each part could be put in the proper place for fitting. The Arabs set up three poles in a tripod and screwed a steel pulley onto the top. Charlie tied one end of the rope around the first section of plywood fuselage and fed the other end through the pulley. The Arabs hauled and the bits of fuselage swung out of their packing and were lowered onto the chalk marks. Next out of the crates came the wings. A team of fitters bolted the plane together and tensioned it with a hydraulic jack. I walked over and pushed on one of the flaps.

'Careful sir,' said Dougie Hatton, a balding man with a broken nose and stained teeth. 'They are real delicate-like. Airbrakes to slow the plane down when we land.' It was disconcerting to me to watch my Horsa being put together on this dusty airstrip as though it was a giant piece of Meccano. But I reminded myself that at least Meccano planes were made out of metal.

We drove back up to the town of Mascara for lunch. The place was like a stage set. There were leafy boulevards but nobody was strolling on them; good shops with nothing in their windows; restaurants with outside tables but no customers; a railway station without any trains and a cinema showing no films. So we went to the hotel bar and when we returned the Arabs had gone and the two sergeants were working on the control lines. I climbed into the fuselage. The top of my head brushed against the roof. The plane was a triumph of the woodworkers' art: the benching was beautifully finished and slightly curved to make it more comfortable. One feature puzzled me. A rubber tube ran up from the floor to a curved metal mouthpiece. I pulled the bung from the mouthpiece and wiggled my finger in the hole.

'What's this for?'

'It's for pissing into, old man. And as for the other, don't ask.'

Peter went into the cockpit. In front of each seat was a metal column with a steering wheel bolted on to it and on the floor was a wooden plank with a leather ring at each end. Peter put his suede boots into the rings. He pushed his right foot forward.

'Turn to port,' he said. The little plank rotated around its middle. 'Now, turn to starboard.'

He pulled the wheel towards him. We heard a twang.

'What the hell do you think you're doing?' shouted an angry voice, 'we haven't connected up the bloody wires yet!'

Peter pointed at a big Thermos bottle with his foot.

'Compressed air to operate the airbrakes. You push this lever with the red knob. The glider will drop like a stone. There's another bottle somewhere for the wheel brakes. Here it is.'

He kicked the second bottle a bit harder.

I walked around the glider. That morning it had been a tumble of crates and now here was a complete fighting machine. I would use it to lead a group of men to war. Metal and rubber for the undercarriage, steel for the control wires, some compressed air but apart from that everything was plywood - a stuff you could kick a hole in with your boot. I looked into one of the big crates turned on its side. A very young soldier sitting on a blanket stared back. He had a pale dirty face with acne and held the barrel of a gun in one hand and a cotton wad in the other.

'We're living in these crates while we build the gliders,' he said. 'Only problem is the niggers thought the bore holes for fresh water were latrines so they're full of shit. Anyway it's a good idea to stay next to the aircraft. Spot of bother last night.' He pointed at the rest of the Sten gun lying on the floor.

'The wogs can take a glider apart in the time it takes to brew up. God knows what they do with the stuff. Still, they're not like us, are they?'

After dinner in the mess we showed photos around. Peter had just put away a snap of his wife and I was passing around one that Douglas Carr had taken.

'The cap hides her hair,' I explained, 'which is all red and crinkly. And you can't appreciate her eyes and her smile because it's slightly blurry. Douglas took it with somebody else's camera and...,' I went on as the other man, whose name was Lawrence Wright, held Bella in his hand.

He took off his spectacles and pretended to be interested in the snapshot. When his turn came he spread out his hands and said, 'I'm a complete fake. Can't even fly a plane. In civvy street I used to be a teacher.' He hurried on before we could ask why he didn't have any snaps to show us.

'I'm in charge of organising the Glider Pilot Regiment. Had a hell of a time getting here. Americans are running the field telephone system and I don't know any of their code names. Eventually I got through to the colonel here and we were just talking when the Yank operator interrupted – Are you through? he asked. So I said – Yes thanks. And he cut me off, just like that. I'm going to have to learn American, I think.' We all laughed but now I think Lawrence was on to something. He was a real intellectual.

'This morning at the requisitioned bank where I work,' Lawrence continued, 'the quartermaster was talking over the telephone with his American opposite number. 'That's right,' he said patiently, 'just so. I need you to move the division's equipment from the railway trucks in Algiers to the lorries.' He stopped to listen then resumed. 'Railroad, sorry, railroad trucks. No, lorries, not trucks. No, not cars. Trucks. I don't understand. What do you mean, ship? I'm talking about a railway – I mean railroad - truck. No, not a truck. A lorry. To the lorries. What is this about ships?' He put the phone delicately back on its cradle as though it might bite him and turned to me. 'The Americans!' he said. 'My lorries are his trucks, my railway trucks he calls railroad cars, and he thinks I have got cars on his trucks. And there's something to do with shipping that I can't get to the bottom of. I hope to God the Jerries have the same problem with Musso or we'll never get this war won.'

The next evening Lawrence and I started work on a pamphlet that put American and English phrases side by side so that both allies could understand what the other was saying. Lawrence called it the book of Babu, for 'British-American book of understanding', and hoped it would be funny to read as well.

I leaned across as he was writing and said, 'I don't like the Yanks calling us all Britishers or Brits. It makes me think of woad.'

'The Scots don't like being called English, Dodo. And be careful about calling all the Yanks Yanks. Some Yanks don't like being called Yanks. They say they're Southerners.'

'I'm an Englishman. That's what we call ourselves in India.'

Lawrence shook his head. 'Listen to what happened to me today, mister Englishman. An American invited me to a meeting on the first floor and then he held it on the ground floor.'

'And if my jeep gets a puncture the Yanks call it a flat. They call flats apartments. Write that down too.'

'Where's Peter this evening?' asked Lawrence.

'He flew back this morning to England, or should I say Britain?' I replied, looking around for the waiter from 'Casablanca'. I had got to like the banana brandy.

'You know he's got a Chinese decoration for flying supplies from Burma over the Himalayas?'

'Why isn't he in Bomber Command instead of transport?'

'We're all rejects one way or another, Dodo. He's too old. I wear specs. You've got a gammy leg. Now let's get on with our book.'

A few days later Lawrence and I moved to a tent on the Froha airstrip and he began to organise transferring the gliders to Tunisia. I was still waiting for my troops. We slept beside the telephone switchboard on camp beds that had belonged to the crew of a Halifax lost towing gliders over. Thieving was our biggest problem. Drums of petrol were too heavy to steal but the Arabs broached them and set them on fire when they had siphoned out everything they could carry. They stole the copper wire so telephones didn't work and communications constantly broke down. The attack was three weeks off and Lawrence put the book of Babu away in his kitbag, but we still shared a few jokes.

Soldiers on the airstrip shot at the Arabs doing the thieving and flogged the ones they caught. I didn't have a problem with this but Lawrence was upset. Instead he had the offender brought in and tried in his pidgin Arabic to make him understand that all this military effort was for his benefit and he should stop sabotaging it. I watched the boy standing in his simple garments rubbing one bare foot against a bare leg and looking with his grave dark eyes at this thin earnest man until he was sent away with a gift of chocolate. At least, Lawrence said to me, I don't think of them as picannies.

13.   Bella's diary

June 15th.

Dodo has sent me a letter. He isn't allowed to say where he is but it is hot and dusty so I guess it can't be too far away. He says that whenever an aircraft takes off it sets up a wall of dust across his camp. At midday red dust-devils thousands of feet high spin across the plain and demolish tents, sending their contents high into the air. He says they can't keep the Arabs out. I can believe that! One of his friends got so angry he fired at a boy with his pistol but the boy was only chasing a donkey that had strayed across the airstrip.

He and his friends have adopted a young man they call the Motor Boy. He stands for hours in the town square making a low throbbing noise from his throat. When he wants to go anywhere he pretends to do the gear shifts in a jeep and holds an imaginary steering wheel in his hands. In top gear he runs down the street tooting to clear pedestrians out of the way.

June 17th.

I'm getting used to death, I think. Deaths on Jutland usually happen at night. Two o'clock in the morning is the commonest time for a patient to depart. The nurses pull red screens around the bed and do their best to keep the dying man quiet. Anyway, I've learned, most men are quiet up to the end. The old sister took me aside last week after I was shocked when a man died silently as I cleaned around his bed.

'Don't judge the severity of a man's pain by the noise he makes,' she said, holding my hand in hers. 'When I was your age at Etaples I learned that the man in real agony won't waste his breath by making complaints. But you are doing well, my dear.'

I've stopped being upset and sometimes they call me down from the dormitory under the roof to help Ahmed bring in the mortuary stretcher, which looks surprisingly like the breakfast trolley with its big wheels. The nurses have stripped and cleaned the body and laid it out with hands crossed and feet straight under a white sheet. Ahmed and I lift the corpse, already stiffening, onto the trolley and take it to the mortuary for burial the next morning.

June 23rd.

Dodo has written to me again. He can't say much so most of the letter is about his friend the Motor Boy. Dodo has given him a real red steering wheel and he goes from table to table in the café asking if anybody would like a lift. If anybody does, Dodo pretends to be a hotel commissionaire and holds the door open while the Motor Boy idles his engine. The soldiers trot behind the Motor Boy and he does a circuit of the square and puts them down in front of their table again. They have to pay him and if they don't shut the door properly, Dodo says the boy steps out of his side of the jeep and slams the door shut before he drives away. Others of Dodo's friends have given him a black chauffeur's cap and a pair of leather gloves.

It sounds terrific fun! I would love to be playing café games like that rather than stuck here cleaning Jutland ward day after day. It is my 19th birthday today but I have nobody to share it with. No word from Papa. Where will I be a year from now?

14.   Flying to Goubrine

Algeria for me is inseparable from memories of the sad figure we used to call the Motor Boy. We were all so bored that we made a great fuss of this crazy young man and his imaginary jeep. Peter even used him to go to the local brothel. The girls leaned out of the window and flung coins at him. Tips were generous and he acquired a complete chauffeur's outfit.. The Motor Bay was very happy with the war until the afternoon came when we moved from the Froha airstrip to Goubrine. It was my first flight in a glider.

'Flaps?' called out Charlie in his Lancashire accent.

'Up,' replied Dougie.

'Air pressure?'

'Two hundred.'

'Trim?'

'Neutral.'

I looked out from the cockpit at Peter's twin-prop Albemarle revving its engines. The towrope was coiled out between us like a giant anaconda snake.

'Tug calling,' came Peter's voice over the intercom sounding as though he was standing at the other end of a field shouting through a towel. 'Hello Matchbox. Are you ready for take-off?'

Charlie grimaced. 'Very funny, Tug. Matchbox here. Ready for take-off.'

The Horsa jerked forward as the towing rope went taut and suddenly the world disappeared in a cloud of red dust blown up by the propellers. The needle of the airspeed indicator was rising: thirty miles per hour, forty, fifty. Sixty miles an hour. Suddenly the big sergeant hauled the control column back. The glider jumped into the air and the dust began to clear. To my horror I saw that the tug plane in front of us was still on the runway. Surely the glider would crash back to earth? But then the tug left the ground and rose above us as the runway slowly receded.

We followed the coastline after we crossed the mountains and I looked for Tabarka and Bella's hospital. I wondered if she might look up at the sky when she heard the planes overhead. But I couldn't find the spot. After four hours in the air, Charlie shouted in my ear, 'Getting close to Goubrine now. Not a moment too soon.' Looking up through the Perspex roof I saw the sky was still a cheerful blue, but down below the villages, roads and groves of palm trees had lost their distinctive outlines. Suddenly two rows of lights shone up from the ground. Dougie jerked his head towards them.

'They've lit the Barton flares to guide us in,' he said and leaned forward over the control panel to cast off the towrope.

Suddenly the glider stopped jerking and a strange silence filled the cockpit. Charlie worked the wooden paddle with his feet until the glider was aligned in the middle of the V-shape made by the two lines of flares. But as I watched one flare and then another went out. In a minute half the flarepath had gone. Charlie was already pushing up the lever to operate the flaps.

'Airbrakes on,' he called.

The ground rushed up to meet us. Just as I thought the aircraft would bury itself in the ground Charlie pulled back on the control stick and the main wheels hit the dirt of the airstrip.

'Wheelbrakes!' shouted Charlie and there was more hissing as the compressed air from the second bottle tightened the callipers around the wheels.

We climbed out and stood in the half-light as a truck drove up. I rubbed my bad leg.

'That went all right,' I said to Dougie, 'but it was quite a moment when those flares started to go out.'

'They didn't go out, the fucking wogs nicked them. Anyway, there won't be any flares when we do the real thing.'

15. Getting Ready

The salt flats where the gliders for the invasion were gathering were a fearsome place to put thousands of young men in: wide bands of dry white salt up to twenty miles long, midway between what was left of the port of Sousse and the holy city of Kairouan on the edge of the mountains. Nothing grew on the pans. At their edges you could see clumps of olive trees, prickly pear bushes and a few tall aloes like lavatory brushes. The aircraft looked like giant dragonflies on the surface of a pond in the mirage of the heat. Everyone lived in tents except Lawrence who had a hut with a wooden floor until Peter pulled the boards up and laid them against the sides so he could pin his maps of the route over Malta. Sergeant Huntley salvaged the seating from crashed Horsas and made a business of cutting holes in the middle and selling them as lavatory seats.

Peter, Lawrence and I were on Goubrine Two. We heard that Goubrine One was better and when Peter and I rode there looking for whisky on a motor bike he'd stolen from somewhere, we understood why. The Americans had built a bar. The bar made it much better and we drank bourbon there most days. Meanwhile the salt pans filled up with men and equipment. The men were British and the equipment was American. American Waco gliders were towed in from Algeria by the Dakotas that still had fuel tanks that did not seal automatically. The Wacos had metal frames covered with canvas like deck chairs. They were roomier and more comfortable than the Horsas but they had small flaps and came down in a shallow glide that took a long time to come to a stop on the ground. They looked like death traps to me. I had heard from Lawrence about Sicily.

Lawrence didn't often get drunk. He didn't like to let go. But one evening we were in the American bar and he asked where they had got the stone flooring. They told him they had paved it with broken headstones from the graveyard in Sousse. That set him off laughing. And then he talked about stone walls.

'The red-faced doctor you told me about, Dodo? The one who said you were going to be travelling like a VIP from now on? He had orders to certify experienced officers like you as fit for glider troops. Even though you know you should have been shipped home. He didn't know why. Do you want to know?'

Peter interrupted. 'Don't tell Dodo about the walls on Sicily, Loll. It's all hush-hush.' He began to laugh as well.

I demanded to know what they were both talking about, although afterwards I wished I hadn't. My fate had been decided a month earlier in a hotel room in Algiers, Lawrence said. The hotel stood on the other side of the busy main road from the harbour, just where the trams turned round. Before the war it had been popular with the merchant captains who made the three day run from Marseilles. The tall windows looked across the main road towards the Liberty ships that filled the port. Despite the open windows and the rotating fan the room was stiflingly hot, and Lawrence said he could hear the noises from the street as he listened to Chatty and the little general arguing. Staff cars purred outside the main entrance and trucks loaded with stores honked as they negotiated their way from the harbour onto the busy road. Donkeys in from the countryside with sacks of carrots and potatoes on their backs brayed unceasingly and on top of all this were human noises: the shouts of their Arab owners and the patter of European tongues, the quick sound of French like scales played on a flute, the thudding of English and the sawing sound of American.

'The general was short ,' Lawrence said, 'with black wavy hair and a moustache. He shook with excitement as he told us that Monty was keen to use his airborne troops to seize bridges and roads before the beach landings started at dawn.'

As the general walked back and forth in front of the map on the wall he jabbed at it with a wooden pointer and lectured them about how important the harbour at Syracuse was. The bridges across the river north of the town had to be taken and held before the enemy could blow them up.

'He jabbed at the road bridge he had codenamed Waterloo Bridge,' said Lawrence, 'so hard that the tip of the pointer went right through the map. Chatty was supposed to get his pilots to land next to the bridges. He pulled out the aerial photographs and spread them across the table. That was when Chatty started to get rattled. I could see it in the way he kept brushing back his hair. 'These fields have stone walls,' he finally said. 'The Horsas are completely made out of wood. If they hit a stone wall they will come apart.' The general just stared at him and said damage to the gliders was acceptable within the plan.'

'So Chatty pointed out his men had no experience of night flying and that he had no tug planes and no airstrips. No difficulty there, the general retorted. The Yanks would build the airstrips and supply the tugs.'

'He meant those Dakotas with the petrol tanks like sieves, Dodo,' said Peter. 'You can think your lucky stars you're flying with my trusty old Albemarle.' He called for another round.

Lawrence ignored him. I could tell he was really upset and wished he had never started to tell me the story. He leaned across the bar and touched my hand. When Chatty started to complain about the American gliders and the stone walls of the landing sites, he said, the general stopped listening to him. He picked up his hat and walked briskly to the door. With one hand on the knob he turned and said he was leaving Chatty for half an hour. At the end of that time Chatty could either agree to the operation or be fired, relieved of his command. There were fourteen divisions and a thousand ships earmarked for the Sicily show, he barked, and it wasn't going to be called off just because colonel

Chatterton was worried about a few stone walls.

When the door had shut, they walked to the window together, lit up and looked over the crowd at the tram stop towards the harbour. A tram went past and the metal wheels of the trams clicked over the joints in the rails: three rapid taps and then the fourth one after a slight delay, like knuckles rapping on a desk. The noise reminded Lawrence of the hammer of a revolver clicking down on the empty chambers. On the other side of the road a column of trucks was heading east for Tunisia.

'Chatty isn't much of a scholar but Hoppy's words about a thousand ships had stuck in his mind. He said he remembered the Greeks had sailed to Troy with a thousand ships. But could the Greeks have come up with another thousand? No doubt the gliders that general Hoppy had talked about were coming over in another thousand ships. And there would be another thousand for the guns and the ammunition and the rations and the chewing gum and planes and gliders and tanks, and many, many men.'

'I knew what he was thinking as we turned over the photographs – they were useless. We needed better recon shots, taken in early morning or evening light when the shadows give you an idea of how high walls are. We could make out the road bridge, crossing what looked like two rivers close together with a canal between. The road ran close to the water. The fields to the south of the bridge were far too small for even the Horsas with their massive flaps and air-brakes to land in. To the north, on the city side of the bridge, there were a couple of bigger fields. And there was a possible landing ground by the railway bridge. He was doing that thing with his hair again. A night assault. Landing an aircraft at night is dangerous. You need weeks of training with instructors and even then it's dangerous.'

Chatty had pushed the photographs around the desk. Perhaps some gliders might land safely but would they be enough for what Hoppy wanted? They stepped back to the window and gazed at the lines of ships covering the horizon as they waited to unload their cargoes and go home for another load.

Lawrence said he suddenly recalled flying down from England two days earlier and gazing fascinated out of the window at Gibraltar. The gut of Gibraltar, the narrow entry from the Atlantic to the Mediterranean, was crowded with shipping. He had given up counting how many vessels lay below on the glistening water. The convoys stretched two thousand miles back across the ocean. And further west the railroads were full of vehicles pouring out of factories all across America. But until that moment, he said, he had not realised what the tentacles were reaching for. This was an octopus, a vast creature coming from the sea to attack Europe. If it was defeated it would recoil briefly and assault with another thousand ships and fourteen divisions.

'The thought staggered me. Then Chatty let me have it. All the emotions inside that unemotional man rose to the surface. He almost wept with frustration. He said that all his life he had been taught to do his duty. If every Englishman did his duty then victory was certain. That was what Nelson's last signal meant. His boarding school was the same one you went to, Dodo. He said he had slept in a dormitory with thirty-five other boys, lashing up and stowing his hammock every morning. He paraded in front of the cadet captain nine times a day. He cheered at the end of each summer term as the passing class marched out through the gates to join the King's armed forces. In the school chapel on Sundays he sat with his friends in the wooden pews and heard the headmaster eulogise the boys who had fallen. The last war ended when he was in his final year and he felt bitterly ashamed at missing the chance to fight. So this war was his second chance. Danger and death came a long way behind. But he wasn't a fool, he said. His glider pilots were relying on him. Hoppy would replace him with somebody who had less experience.

The attack would still go ahead.'

The barman had set up another round. I looked at the slabs beneath my feet.

'He didn't have a choice,' I replied.

'On the other hand, the plan is mad. Hoppy is mad. He wants his troops to be used early because he is scared they may not be used at all, and that would be the end of his career. He doesn't care about casualties. He may even welcome them if they mean glory and medals.'

'But that's not my business. My business is to do my duty.' I felt sick.

'Yes, that's what Chatty said. When the door opened and general Hoppy walked in Chatty turned away from the window and faced him, smiling and saying, 'Thank you for giving me the opportunity to study the photographs, sir. Please tell me about the part the gliders will play in as much detail as possible.' The general opened a drawer and took out a bottle and three glasses. At the end he was even ready to make a joke. But Hoppy paid enough attention to understand that a lot of men would be killed. He said he would put one officer with combat experience into each glider so at least one experienced officer would get to the bridges. And that is the story of how you ended up in gliders, Dodo.'

The evenings in the bar with my two friends were the best times. The intense heat of midday spread like a stain to infect the mornings and the evenings. It stopped being cool for a few hours after midnight. The crayons in the operations hut melted and the red marking on Peter's maps bled across the surface of the Mediterranean. At 120 degrees in the shade the air over the pans was so thin that the gliders could not get enough lift to take off. The Dakotas and Halifaxes could only fly in the early morning and the evening. So Huntley and I trained our men on the ground, packing them into a glider which Dougie and Charlie pretended to take into the air.

In the furnace of Goubrine the exercises quickly grew exhausting.

Huntley couldn't cope with the heat. So he made mistakes and one morning died when he was showing a group of soldiers how to handle grenades. One of the men dropped a grenade after he had taken out the pin. Huntley threw himself on top of it before it exploded. Nobody else was hurt. The affair depressed me. Huntley had been wrong to try to train that calibre of men with a live grenade. So I promoted Smith in his place.

I would have run away myself, I thought at the time. The truth was that Huntley had fought at Alamein and I liked him. If Huntley could be killed in a stupid accident, what hope was there for me? And I wanted to live so much for Bella's sake.

16.   Scuffy Lintle

I hadn't received any letters from Bella, although I wrote to her most days. I dreamed a lot about her. As I said, I am one of those people who can remember dreams almost as intensely as real life: their colour, their smells and the feelings in them. When I dream I remember all my other dreams going back to when I was a boy so that I really inhabit a dream world as I sleep. Now I kept dreaming that I was back in the hospital at Tabarka but I couldn't find Bella. Douglas was helping but it was no good. Every time I went to Jutland she had just gone off duty or was elsewhere in the hospital. Huntley was in the bed behind the red screens and he knew where Bella was but I didn't dare pull the screens aside.

One morning I borrowed a jeep and drove off the airstrip. I wanted to find a piece of land that was flat and empty, sit in the middle of it and try to forget about Sicily and those damned walls. My jeep eventually came to a major road. Both sides were lined with peach and fig trees. Fruit was ripening on them and wicker baskets stood beside the trunks but nobody was about. In the distance I could see a few figures working in the fields. The thought struck me that in Africa the dead season was the summer. Winter was short and rainy: autumn and spring were the growing times. But the summer gave nothing to this land.

There were convoys of vehicles stretching as far as I could see in either direction. In the dust, olive-painted columns of American trucks passed British ones in sandpaint. Four motor-bikes escorting a staff-car flew by with sirens blaring. Beside the road were compounds surrounded by wire with prisoners sitting inside them. Other prisoners were filling in the holes in the road left by shellfire. The roadside was littered with wrecked trucks. From time to time I saw burnt-out planes and vehicles between the fig and peach trees.

I swung onto an unpaved track that wound between lines of eucalyptus with white peeling trunks and dirty light-green leaves before it emerged onto a plain bounded by a line of sand dunes with the sea beyond. In the middle distance was a group of military vehicles. As I came closer I realised they were the wrecks of jeeps, trucks and gun carriers. Suddenly a horn blared and a jeep overtook me and came to a stop right in my path. A Sikh with a high turban secured by a large red ring came to attention and saluted me.

I followed him round the other side of the vehicles to a camp. A large Englishman with a moustache got up from a trestle table. The man had a black patch over one eye and a tweed fishing hat on his head. The hat had once been brown but was now grey with age. The crown was festooned with salmon flies made up with black silk. Most were brown or red and I recognised an Orange Parson and a purple Rosy Dawn among them. The flies were firmly hooked into the tweed cloth but as the man shook his head the trailing threads moved with the motion so that it seemed he was looking through cobwebs. He had a major's crowns on the shoulders of his battledress top. Coloured crayons were poking out of his chest pockets, but the fishing motif reasserted itself below with green plus fours and socks ending in a highly polished pair of brown brogues. We shook hands, the man smiling broadly. He was missing the middle finger.

'Sorry about this,' said the apparition. 'We thought you were the sky pilot bringing over the maps. Never mind, we'll just troll with what we've got. Now you're here though, have a cup of tea.'

I stared at him. Where on earth had we met before?

'It's Scuffy Lintle,' I said after a moment. The man jerked his head to one side and observed me closely through his left eye. Then he closed it, lifted up his eye patch and did the same thing again with his right eye. This disconcerted me as the eye was milky white and surrounded by scarred and inflamed tissue. Scuffy seemed to realise what he was doing and flipped the patch down.

'Force of habit, I'm afraid,' he said. 'But it is Dodo Deeds isn't it?

When did we last meet? Cairo? Alex? Kore's House?'

'What are you doing here? I thought they'd shipped you back to England.'

'Not a chance,' replied Scuffy, twirling the thread connected to the Orange Parson around his finger, 'not with JW at a fiver a bottle. Anyway what could I do? Far better to be in the gravediggers' brigade. Clean air, bright light and the prospect of some decent angling if the war goes on.'

I looked around. Men were hauling equipment out of the backs of the trucks. Long-handled spades were stacked against their sides, next to what looked like the sort of spears used to stick pigs in India.

'Have a cup of tea. Perhaps the padre will turn up eventually.'

We sat down at the trestle table and an Indian messboy produced mugs of tea. Scuffy poured whisky into both, leaned back in his chair and took a good pull. He waved his hand at the camp. 'I run an empire, Dodo' he said. 'You think it's hard to kill people? It's nothing to the effort we trollers put in to fishing them out of the sands again. We carry everything in the trucks - wooden crosses, metal punching machine for the labels, white paint for the stones to mark the graveyard. '

'How did I get into this sport? You heard I stepped on an S-mine at Alamein. After they'd patched me up I was moved into some filthy hotel in Cairo, all ready to be plonked into the next boat. Haven't been back to England since '34. Then one evening in the bar I ran into a colonel. Much the same shape I was in - one eye gone, bits of tin all over his body. We fell to talking and he said he could arrange for me to stay out as one of his trollers. He ran the graves registration service for the whole of Eighth Army.' He poured out more whisky.

'The colonel needed a burial officer for 4th Indian Div. Last chap who had the job hadn't realised he was in a minefield. Nothing left of him. His sepoys couldn't find enough to put in a burlap sack. Couldn't even take advantage of his own service. Funny really. But the point was, I had combat experience. I knew what a bloody minefield looked like. He said he would put me into a major's uniform and send me into the desert with 80 sepoys at a day's notice. The boat for Durban was leaving in two days. It was up to me to decide. We were rather merry by this time. You love to fish, he said. Work for me and I will make you a fisher of men. Ha!'

'Sorry to bother you sir, but there is another argument going on between the Moslems and Hindus.'

It was the Sikh sergeant-major. Scuffy stood up.

'Come along Dodo, I'll show you how complicated this job is,' he said.

Two soldiers, one short and one tall, were leaning over a hole. A third was standing in the hole with a piece of cloth in his hand. The small man began, 'These are the remains of a Hindu soldier, Sahib, who should...'

The tall man interrupted him.

'I beg to differing. My assistant has just unearthed a piece of clothing with a text from Holy Koran stitched into it.'

The worker in the grave passed the cloth up and the excitable sergeant waved it in front of the other's face.

The little man's expression did not change. 'Cloth and writings may have come from anywhere, dear colleague,' he said in a precise voice. 'The soldier who lies here before us has the tattoo mark of the chakra or wheel of fate on his neck. This is proof positive that he is a Hindu, of the Bengali caste who have themselves embroidered precisely for the purpose of distinctiveness in such a situation.'

I wondered what Scuffy would say in reply but he didn't respond. Instead he took off his fishing hat, handed it to the Sikh and flipped up his eyepatch. The soldiers went rigid, their gazes fixed on the dead right eye. He took the piece of cloth and held it in front of the eye. Leaning forward he moved his head to side from side over the hole, then straightened up, replaced the eyepatch, and put the tweed hat back on. The Indians relaxed.

'It is clear as daylight, sergeant Dass, that the dead man is indeed a Hindu, of the Bengali caste. Therefore I authorise you to take the body up and place it ready for burning. Sergeant Madass, you are also correct in believing that the remains of a Moslem man are close by. You will continue trolling the area until you find him.'

We walked back to the table. The sun was setting and the burned-out vehicles of the Indian division cast long shadows eastwards towards us.

'The blind peeper comes in useful in these situations,' said Scuffy. 'Quite the evil eye as far as these lads are concerned. They won't dare argue when I deploy the eye at them. It still hurts like hell though. They say that if you lose a foot you feel that it's there on the end of your leg. Sometimes when I'm lying awake in the tent this eye takes on a life of its own. I see things with it. Places I can't remember ever having been to: rivers in Kashmir I've never fished, nightclubs I've never danced in, dusky maidens I've never shagged.'

The messboy produced a fresh bottle of Johnny Walker. Scuffy seemed to have forgotten about me as he continued musingly, 'The Arabs steal from the graves. Boots especially. Take a look at the footwear of your typical Arab and you'll find he's wearing army boots. But the real problem in this job is our wogs. How can you always sort out which type of wog you've turned up? There are 200 separate races or religions or faiths in the Indian army and we've got most of them in 4th Div. Gurkhas, Jats, Pathans, Dogras, Rajputs, Mahrattas, Sikhs, Madrassis, Bengalis, even the odd Parsee. Parsees are the worst. They want to be left up top on a platform so the birds can eat them.'

He laughed again, a short barking sound.

'That's happened a lot anyway before we get on site. But it's the Hindus and the Moslems are the main problem, as you know from India. Hindus want to be burned. Moslems want to be left where they fell. Warrior ideal. So you shouldn't dig up a Moslem and you have to dig up a

Hindu. That was what Dass and Madass were arguing about. I give them a burst of the evil eye and half the time tell them it's a Hindu, and the other half that it's a Moslem.'

A jeep drew up and a tired man in soiled uniform with white crosses on his lapels came across to the table. 'Can't stop long, Scuffy. Here's the map. Make sure you give it back. I buried nine - no, ten - of our men over there.' He pointed with his mug.

'What did you do about the Jerries?'

The padre shrugged. 'Common grave. You can see the mound if you walk towards the sea a bit. Now I must be off. Having a memorial service back at brigade this evening. Div is being held back for R&R in the Lebanon.'

Scuffy took off his hat and ran his hand through his brown hair as the chaplain drove away. He fingered one of the lures. 'There's a bit of carp fishing in the Lebanon' he said. 'They might even find the odd mahseer in the Litani – no trout though. I'm looking forward to Italy, if that's where we're attacking next. Sardinia's a wash-out but there are a few rivers in Sicily. There's the Anapo that runs by Syracuse. The Gela, the Salso, but they won't have much water in them at this time of year. Fished out too, probably. But the Grande is worth a try. Should be some eels at least. Sergeant-major, the padre buried the Jerries in a common grave. Take some men with pig-sticks and troll around a bit over there.'

The light was fading fast now and I had no wish to go back to the aerodrome so I leaned on my elbows and watched Scuffy dressing flies. It was clearly a nightly ritual. He brought out a small wooden cabinet and took out a pair of scissors, a large darning needle and a small pair of pliers. From another drawer he laid on the table next to the lamp a pair of surgeon's forceps and a knife. The mess-boy brought a tin plate with petrol in it.

'Got to keep your fingers clean when you're working with wax.'

He took a fish hook and length of gut and with his left hand jabbed the hook into the map's surface. Then he twisted the gut tightly around the hook, tensioning it with his damaged right hand. He passed over a small ball of wax.

'Help me by warming some wax, will you? Just rub it between your finger and thumb until it gets soft while I wind out the silk.'

Scuffy pressed the warm wax onto the map and ran the silk thread through it from end to end, laying it on the table when he had finished. Then he put his fingers into the mess-tin and wiped them on his dirty tunic.

'Now this is the tricky bit, especially if you're a finger short- winding the silk around the gut.'

All at once, I was startled by a bang and a sheet of flame. As the flames died down I saw a pile of bodies burning on a heap of smashed vehicles. I walked towards the funeral pyre. The little Hindu Dass was walking counter-clockwise around the fire chanting softly and holding a long wooden stick in his hand.

'The major allows us a ration of petrol. It is all topsy-turvy, Sahib, but we do our best. There is no holy kusha grass to light the fire, and I must do it myself as there are no untouchables inside the division, despite their usefulness in dirty business of this kind.'

The smell was in my nostrils and I walked away into the desert to look at the stars. When I came back to the table Scuffy was examining quills of bird feathers.

'Shot a bustard two days ago,' he said. 'Great piece of luck I had the Bren with me. Couldn't ask for better hackles.'

Very delicately and firmly he wound the quill around the gut and silk covering the body of the fish hook. At the base of the hook he tied the feathers on again with silk, cut the rest of the quill off, and teased out the feathers with his darning needle until they plumped up. He put his materials back in the cabinet and folded the maps away.

'Pity about the wax and holes in these staff maps. The way I look at it is there isn't likely to be a fly-fishing shop in Tunis or Sicily, so I have been making all my own flies. A brown dun like this will always come in handy. Another whisky?'

Over supper Scuffy explained his views to me on the future course of the war. They revolved around angling. Invading Sardinia was pointless: a strategic dead-end with no fly-fishing at all and Greece was not much better, although you could get decent fishing in other parts of the Balkans. Italy was the most likely choice. Certainly there were carp and bream in the Italian rivers, provided the Allies moved rapidly before the hungry locals could dynamite out the streams. Scuffy wasn't hopeful.

'Our generals have no imagination. The Jerries will be waiting for us in Sicily. What we should do is what Herr Hitler doesn't expect. I'll draw a map to explain what I mean.'

He pulled out a crayon.

'Look at the shape of the Italian boot, Dodo. It's perfect for a Jerry defence. Take us years to reach a decent river. Yet over at Gibraltar we could be in southern Spain in a couple of hours. And best of all, the Spanish are neutrals so brother Jerry won't be expecting us to attack.'

Mister Lintle had fished in Spain before the first war and Scuffy carried his father's fishing diary everywhere he went. He turned over the pages under the light of the pressure lamp. In the south the Guadalquivir had shad and swarmed with eels. The river Bonar trout were famous in Leon, and there was splendid otter-hunting. At Las Pearas his father had caught trout of huge proportions in the pools, but they would not take a fly easily.

'Blue duns or March brown. This bustard fly would attract them. Orange duns in the Ancora. Partridge flies perhaps, though God knows where we'd get partridges in the middle of a war.'

Sergeant-major Sikh laid a bundle on the table.

'We found the Germans where the reverend indicated, Sahib.'

Scuffy spilled out several tins the size of sardine cans. I picked one up. Inside was what looked like a small toothpaste tube with a needle at one end.

'Morphine injectors, standard Wehrmacht issue. Frontline soldiers, for the use of. Not like our lot where only the paramedics are allowed to carry Omnipon.'

'I've come across dead Germans with morphine on them. But I've never seen this many before from just a few soldiers.'

'The Jerries put them in their socks. The Eyeties put the tins down their underwear, but I think the Jerries have the right idea. Makes sense if you think about it. A tin goes in each sock, so even if one leg gets blown off you still have enough morphine in the other one to do the business. This is a good haul though. Worth a lot of money on the black market.'

But Scuffy shook his head. He could tell what I was thinking.

'They're the icing on the cake for me. This damned eye of mine hurts like blazes. A Berlin pharmaceutical is just what I need to get a decent night's sleep. I've been running low.'

He held out his damaged right hand. The tin fell through the hole where the middle finger should have been but Scuffy caught it deftly with his other hand before it disappeared into the darkness.

'Boy, get another bottle of JW from my tent. I'll be back in a minute or two.'

Later in the evening the Sikh joined us. We talked about fishing in India: the sacred fish of the Vedas, the mighty mahseer in the stony runs and pools of the Himalayas which would only take a fly with a lot of black or peacock harl in it. The sergeant-major spoke of catching snow trout on the Afghan border.

'At Fort Chakdarra in the winter you must fish from the fort garden, where four trees stand on the river bank near the ruined cemetery. It is A-1 fishing there on a blackamoor fly.'

Scuffy was explaining the best way to catch a crocodile when Dass appeared with his wooden club and asked permission to release the souls of the dead.

'Carry on sergeant Dass,' cried Scuffy in a merry voice. 'Crack the Gordian nut. Haha!'

'Kapalakriya. The sergeant will release the trapped souls from their bodies.' The Sikh too had become very drunk.

I watched Dass pulling the pyre apart with a pig-stick. When he found a skull Dass rolled it to one side and shattered it into pieces with a single blow.

The next morning I awoke with a headache. Scuffy was still snoring. He had covered his good eye with the eyeshade and the dead eye observed me as I dressed. Outside the tent the encampment was already busy. Men were getting up from morning prayer. Further away teams were unearthing the bodies which the trollers had found with their pig-sticks on the previous day. Madass was marking out the burial ground with white stones. A heap of blackened metal showed where last night's funeral pyre had been, but the shattered skulls and bones were gone.

As I drove back I pondered on what Scuffy had said about wogs – our wogs and their wogs. It gave me my first inkling of the Europeans' isolation in this land. What would happen if we ever lost this certainty that we know what we want to happen next, and they don't? I thought, and from that moment on I couldn't help noticing how many Arabs had army boots on their feet.

17.   Bella's diary

June 29th.

Dodo has been writing me lots of letters. They come every day in brown envelopes with the mark of the censor on them. He doesn't say where he is or what he is doing so he fills the paper with how much he loves me. I daren't reply. It would come out false. Better to say nothing than be caught lying, Mama used to say.

Today we packed up the ward and propped all the beds against the walls. The ground floor has already been taken over by the military and transport planes had been arriving all day. Tomorrow or the next day everything will be put on the trucks. Poticare says we are going to Sicily but it is a secret. I was standing on the veranda and looking up at the aeroplanes. Suddenly he jabbed me. 'What a pinchable bottom you have, auxiliary nurse,' he said. I said nothing but forced a smile onto my face. He took my hand and kissed it. He is so loathsome!

He said he was inviting me to a very special dinner for our last night at Tabarka. The hospital is becoming a headquarters and generals are arriving. Women were needed to welcome them and he, Poticare, had put himself in charge of supplying ladies. He told me the guest of honour was Winston Churchill himself...or at least I think that's what he said. He kept moving towards me with his mouth open. I know that look and I retreated along the veranda. Won't it be exciting to meet the British Prime Minister!

Later

The dinner was held in the old refectory. I sat on one side of Poticare and his current girlfriend sat on the other. Opposite me was a small general with a dyed black moustache. I looked around for Winston Churchill but couldn't see him. Still, I thought, probably Winston Churchill will come in later. He is very busy winning the war. I was more concerned about trying to eat my dinner while fending off Poticare's hand under the table. I had no idea what the man across from me was saying. Suddenly the general stopped talking. He lifted up his knife. Leaning across the table he jabbed it hard at the doctor's chest. A small splash of gravy appeared on Poticare's shirt. The hand between my legs was instantly withdrawn. 'Stop it, you disgusting man,' said the general. 'I am talking to this young lady.'

When the dinner was over we had coffee in the garden and a circle gathered around a man in civilian clothes. The kind general, who spoke good French and told me his name was Hopkinson, said it was Mister Macmillan, Winston Churchill's personal representative. They were listening to him talk about the world after the war. Mister Macmillan thinks that a permanent alliance between England and America is the way forward. He says the Americans are like the Romans. They have immense power but no subtlety and above all no vision of what they want the world to become. He says England's power is in decline but the English have the wisdom that comes from centuries of empire. The English have the culture, the education, above all the understanding of how to rule. They just have to find out what the Americans want to do next before they know it themselves, he said, then put it forward as their own suggestion. Adjusted to suit the English interests, of course.

He stopped talking for a moment and somebody offered him a cigarette. The flame flared against his spectacles and tired hooded eyes. I thought he was a bit of an actor and wished to make a theatrical pause. He carried on talking: 'Do you know what Winston Churchill has called the Americans? 'That numerous and talkative people....' is how the Prime Minister describes them.'

The little general and I moved in closer. I had heard the words 'Winston Churchill' and thought perhaps the great man was about to appear at last. A long finger was waved in a disapproving way at Macmillan, like the way the teachers used to reprimand me at school. At the other end of the finger stood a thin man with a pencil moustache.

'The Romans conquered the Greeks and made them slaves. Are you suggesting we should offer to become slaves of the Americans, Minister? Our cousins are in some ways not friends at all. They want us to get rid of our Empire. That's not very friendly. We will end up as the 49th state of America.'

Macmillan turned back to the group. 'This is colonel Powell,' he explained, 'and he may have a point. Certainly the British and Americans are two peoples divided by a common language. How often have you asked for a glass of whisky out here and been handed bourbon instead? I always say that I would like a JW and soda to avoid confusion. How kind! It wasn't a hint, you know.'

It was an amusing conversation. But I had given up hope of meeting Winston Churchill the Prime Minister. Now I guessed Poticare just said that he was coming to make sure I went along.

We sat down on a bench. The general said he had enjoyed the dinner and I was the sweetest thing he had seen since he left England. I thought: here we go, but it wasn't like that at all. He wanted to talk. What a strange man. He told me how much he loved war and fighting. He wasn't impressed by what Macmillan had said. He had no time for the Greeks and Romans idea. It was just the sort of thing a politician would come up with, he thought. Generals understood that warfare and running an empire was not about ideas, it was about equipment. His great insight from his friendship with the Americans was that they only cared for material things. They liked to talk but they were quickly bored and nothing bored them faster than ideas. The new American world would not be an age of ideas. There had been too many: communism, fascism and the rest. What the Americans called their ideas were only justifications of their own self-interest, the general said. This would be a material age and the key to the Anglo-American partnership was equipment. Sicily was the perfect example (I was amazed that he talked so much to me about the invasion). He is in charge of the gliders. So I suppose he is Dodo's boss. The Americans are providing most of the tug planes and gliders. He is providing the men. The Americans have come up with the fuel but the plan is British.

He told me that everywhere the Americans go in Africa they have machines that cool the air. They call them 'gizmos', he says. They force the air over cold water and that cools it down. It takes a lot of fuel to run the gizmos but the Americans don't worry about that. He says they have ice-cream at every meal and they eat steaks and leave a lot of the meat on the side of the plate when they've finished. It's hard to believe but he swears it's true. He says that after the war he's going to make sure the English buy lots of gizmos and use them out in India, where it's even hotter than here.

June 30th.

Early this morning I went out for a walk by myself, up the hill behind the hospital to where the ruins of the Greek temple are. Just a few stones, barely one on top of another, but it gives me a feeling of peace when I stand there and look at the mountains and think that Papa is on the other side. Only today I looked the other way at the sea and tried to guess where Sicily lies. I wasn't watching where I was going on the way back and suddenly I realised a twig by my foot had moved so I stopped. It was a puff adder. I've never seen a puff adder before but I knew what it was when I saw its grey skin and white rings. I screamed out loud but I didn't dare move. The snake lifted its head and looked at me lazily, as though it was wondering whether to take a bite out of me or not. I don't know how long the adder and I stared at one another- only twenty or thirty seconds, most likely. A stone landed nearby and with a quick movement the snake slithered off the path. I almost fell down out of fright. But somebody caught me and helped me up and asked me if I had been bitten. It was the tall thin colonel who was sitting next to Mister Macmillan at dinner. He was out of breath from running up the hill. He took me the few steps back to the temple and sat me down on a stone and took out his handkerchief so I could wipe my face. I only pretended to use it because it was quite grubby.

The colonel gave me a cigarette and started to talk about how interesting the temple site was, to calm me down I think. Then I asked him if he was an archaeologist and I talked about my town. When he found out where I came from he got excited and said he had always wanted to visit the mosaics. Did I know about any Etruscan inscriptions there? I began to talk about the mosaic of Orpheus charming the wild beasts and how Papa had been in the excavations and then he sat down and told me almost his whole life story. Well, the bits about archaeology anyway. He's an expert on the Etruscans. So I asked him what he was doing in the army. He replied that the army had had no idea what to do with a professor of archaeology who spoke fluent Italian and possessed a mind like a filing cabinet (he is proud of this boast and told me twice).

So the army made him a paymaster for the troops. The safe with the cash was in the back of his truck and he towed a small gun. Nobody knew how to fire it. They only knew it mustn't be lost. They only had one encounter with the enemy. In a small desert town that both sides believed was behind their front lines the pay truck turned into the main square and nearly hit a Tiger tank. The driver accelerated around the square while the corporal leaned out of the window and gave a running commentary. The colonel said it was like watching the Grand National, which is an English horse race. The Jerries were standing up, the corporal told him. They were staring at the truck. They were running towards their tank. They were climbing into their tank. They were starting the engine. They were traversing the gun barrel. And then the truck was out of the square. He said that after that episode the army took the truck with the safe and the gun away from him and promoted him to colonel with the Allied military government of Italy. He is very happy and hopes it will be somewhere with classical remains to investigate.

The two of us walked down the hill as he was telling me all this and he took me into the officer's mess and gave me a cup of sweet tea and a biscuit. In the Oxford common rooms his colleagues call him 'Sticky'. We both laughed at that because he does look like a long jointed stick insect and his trousers end midway up his bony ankles. He has a slight stoop and fingernails stained yellow with nicotine from the cigarettes he chain-smokes. He looks as though he has missed a day's shaving and not washed that morning, just like some of the professors who used to come to the museum from Paris. We are going for a stroll to the temple this evening before supper.

Later.

Sticky is not unattractive. He is tall and wiry with a strong profile and good skin. His teeth are yellowed by years of smoking but he still has a full set. He must be very old – at least forty – because he was telling me about his excavations twenty years ago and the day the Etruscans began to fascinate him. We climbed up to the temple by a steeper path because Sticky wanted to make sure we avoided where the adder frightened me. He said it reminded him of walking up the steep little streets of Corneto with the workmen pushing their wheelbarrows to the Etruscan site, past the old church and out through the walls towards the city of the dead. The graves were scattered all over the hillside that had been cleared of crops and smelt of nothing except dust and dry grass. On this particular morning that he wanted to tell me about, a party of English visitors arrived to look at the tombs. A little man with a russet beard like the pelt of a fox came over to where Sticky was working. His face was shockingly thin and his eyes glittered. He was writing a book about the ancient Etruscans.

He said that the paintings in these tombs celebrated life, men and women drinking and dancing and loving together. There was no fear of death, only the joy of life. Even the so-called pornographic paintings of whippings and homosexuality were joyous. As the man spoke he spat into an envelope and folded it neatly back in the pocket of his jacket.

Sticky told him that he was sorting through the bits of pottery for their writing. We had first to understand the language. Until then it was like dealing with cave paintings. The author put on his dark glasses and replied that he was interested in what the paintings told him about the Etruscans' zest for love and their uninhibited attitude to sex. He left the language to the academics.

That same day the workmen found a new tomb. Sticky ran across the field but he was too late of course. When his eyes had adjusted to the glare of the acetylene torches he saw he was standing in a large oblong chamber. On three sides there were stone couches on which figures lay. The clothing and flesh had crumbled and he could see the marks in the dust where jewellery had been stolen. The foreman grabbed his arm and Sticky said he smelled his foul breath.

Together they gazed at the walls in silence. The tomb was painted as a canopy against the heat of a summer day and the Etruscan party was in full swing. Above the corpses on their benches were painted figures lying on carved wooden beds, propped up on their elbows and gazing at the entertainment. Naked boys in red ochre with nut-brown hair poured wine from great jugs. In the distance were the animals of the forest and orange birds like cockatoos. Blonde girls in chiffon dresses were dancing on the far wall and a male figure with a massive erection stood to one side. His head was covered by the mask of a bull and his body was painted red. In one hand he held out a white egg, the symbol of life. The painting was extraordinarily graceful. Sticky told me that for the first time he wondered if he was right to concentrate on the language. Even without their language, he thought, we might learn more from the pictures. Over the next few days the colours faded. The blues and greens and oranges were the first to go. Red ochre was more resistant so that it seemed to him the naked man stood still while around him the women, the musical instruments and the forest creatures disappeared as in the ending of a dream. The egg itself disappeared completely.

Sticky finished his story and looked at me as though he wanted me to give him some sort of answer. When I smiled he said, 'If only I had stared for a few minutes longer on that first morning I feel I could have walked through a door into the world of the Etruscans. But that chance has passed me by. I will walk you back to the hospital. You are all leaving for Bizerta this evening. The invasion is definitely on.'

18.   Captain Tex

I felt sorry for the Texan captain in charge of base security in the last days before we invaded. He couldn't defend Goubrine from the Arabs because there was no barbed wire. He told me that his grandfather had made a living from barbed wire in all its hundred types, first from Joe Glidden's patented wire, then Howie's Waco coil with its single thick strand and the twin barbs and the U.S. concertina wire that had been sold in thousands of miles during the last war.

'If I could get enough concertina wire to put around this airstrip my troubles would be over,' he complained. 'But you know what they say about the U.S. Army: not enough or too much, either too big or too small.'

At night the Barton flares that marked the airstrip kept disappearing. Jeeps were found in the morning propped up on wooden blocks with their wheels and tyres gone. When trucks approached the base they would often be halted by a flock of sheep crossing the road. The driver would shout abuse at the old shepherd who waved his arms and shook his head as though to say, 'These sheep have a mind of their own. I can do nothing with them.' A gang of small boys would meanwhile jump up from where they had been hiding by the side of the road. The most common losses were food, but boxes of ammunition and rifles were also taken. So the captain put up a sign in English and French forbidding trucks to halt outside the base.

One afternoon when Peter and I came back from drinking bourbon at the bar with the gravestones, men from the village wearing British army boots were standing in the road talking to the Texan. He asked us if we understood what the villagers were saying. 'A lorry has knocked somebody down,' said Peter, 'a child.' The captain shook his head.

'You mean a truck,' he replied. 'Happened a couple of hours ago. Kid wouldn't get out of the way. They can read the sign.'

We stared at him.

'Tell them I'm sorry about the kid. I guess we'd better go along with them.'

The village stood in a patch of dusty green next to a grove of date palms with a well. Everywhere there was rubbish: animal bones and skulls, bits of burlap sacks, dried-out corn cobs, broken chairs and crockery and rotten pieces of harness.

The walls were made of dried mud and palm fronds had been used as roofing. Dogs sat in the dust outside the doors and scratched themselves. The door frames were made from palm trunks and the doors had shapes painted on them: circles and star patterns and the outline of hands in red paint.

Wrapped in a linen sheet, the dead boy was lying in an open coffin in a downstairs room surrounded by women. They were bending low to the ground and making a rapid sound like the fire of a machine gun with their tongues. 'Allah, Allah, Allah, Allah,' they chanted. Their black cloaks reminded me of the first time I met Bella. Outside the captain fetched a roll of money out of his pocket to pay for the boy. It was not easy because the men had no idea of what a dollar was worth. The captain gave them ten one-dollar bills and two fives. He put the roll away and took a pack of Chesterfields and handed them round. Each of the men took two Chesterfields and the captain gave the rest to the man who had the money. But later that evening a guard post came under fire from the direction of the village and the captain put in a phone call to Sousse.

Next night we had another big exercise. At the tents Peter left his crew and came to tell me what he had seen from the air. We decided to find the Texan captain. In the light of the bike's headlamps we picked out a group of young men in khaki uniforms and headscarfs. The Arabs had rifles in their hands and bandoliers of cartridges over their shoulders. In his tent the captain was drinking beer. He sat on the edge of his bed and listened to Peter, rubbing the skin on his high forehead with one hand while he held a bottle of beer in the other. When Peter finished the captain opened more beers.

'Sure I know about the village getting bulldozed today,' he replied. 'Don't you worry about the folks. We put them in trucks and sent them down to Sousse with all their things. Even put the goddamn animals in trucks and sent them down to Sousse. They'll be looked after. Bet you they'll get some medical attention too: clean them up, the kids will get their shots.'

Peter drank the beer and looked at him. 'You tore down all the palm trees,' he said. It will take twenty years to grow more. Twenty years from now is 1963.'

'They can apply for compensation. Hell, I bet half of them won't even want to come back,' he said. 'I'm only going to say this once and then let's shake hands like partners and try to get some sleep. We're invading Europe in 24 hours. Uncle Sam didn't ask to be involved in this war.' The captain belched. 'Our war is against the Japs. Hitler never bombed Pearl Harbour. I'm here to get this mess sorted out and go home. The British, the French, you're fighting for your lives. Forget the fucking British Empire.'

'We're supposed to be allies,' I complained.

'You Britishers are so poor we have to supply you with everything, the food you eat, the booze you drink, the paper you wipe your assholes with. Yeh, I bet even the wood for those gliders you fly came from States-side, courtesy of Uncle Sam.'

'I passed a jeep full of wogs with rifles on the way,' Peter said.

'I'm not sitting on my ass while soreheads shoot into my base because they think twenty bucks wasn't enough compensation. So we've hired some extra protection. I don't care what happens after we leave. Maybe the Frenchies will be more careful now some of them have guns.'

Peter and I looked at the captain. He was in the right, we knew that. Nobody had been hurt apart from the boy and he had probably been a thief. Somebody had certainly fired into the base last night. I could have been killed lying asleep on my bed. The locals were better off eating fried chicken in Sousse while a nurse gave them injections against typhus. It hurt to have these facts stated so baldly but that was what you expected from the Americans.

The captain reached for more bottles. Peter spoke about his time in China and I said a few words about India and the captain talked about killing cattle. He had worked in the stockyards at Fort Worth and knew about cattle. The longhorns came on their own hooves, in long lines filing into the pens before dawn so that they were still full of water from the drinking troughs.

'Those damned farmers like to sell them with the weight of the water still inside them.'

He remembered wondering as a boy why the cattle in the pens never gored each other with their long horns, some of them five feet across from tip to tip.

'Pa used to say they're peaceable beasts. You and me, we'd fight back, but they go quietly. They be scared as hell though.'

The cattle were sold by the pen at so many cents a pound, and weighed on a great scale like a steel truck. Out the other side was the tunnel that led to the Armour plant. The tunnel wound like a serpent, slowing the beasts down and separating them into single file until the man with the bolt machine split their skulls and his mates hoisted the carcasses onto hooks for processing. The whole assembly line took an hour from buying a steer to rendering it into sides of beef ready to go north in the refrigerated rail cars.

Business had always been steady. Even in hard times people wanted to eat red meat. A war was the best time of all. The armies marched on meat; canned meat for the soldiers, steaks for the officers.

'Sometimes now at chow time I wonder if the beef is from a steer I bought. Probably once in a while it is,' he said, tilting his face back to catch the last drops of beer. The demand for meat was so great that Fort Worth became known as the Wall Street of Beef. He met a lady who worked in one of the new smoke houses that Armour had built and stopped going to the bars that advertised cold beer and hot women.

'But then,' and he spat on the ground, 'the Army called me up. So off I went one wet morning. Climbed on the bus at Exchange Street. Rolling away from the business of killing steers and into the business of killing people, I guess.'

Peter and I finished our beers and said goodnight. The captain went to sleep, I suppose. He certainly had a clean conscience. I never saw him again but I've often thought about him. Did he ever remember Goubrine and the death of the little boy? For years his work had been to select beasts for slaughter and perhaps he believed that the fact he never meant to kill the boy let him off the hook. But he should have known that on an individual level most killing is random. Anyway, the next morning we had our formal briefing on the invasion and were officially told we were invading Sicily. I lay on my bed in the afternoon holding my bowels in check and wondering whether to write Bella a final letter. When I went for a short walk a klaxon horn made me jump out of the way of an ambulance as it headed up the airstrip, weaving between the rows of aircraft and gliders that were filling up with troops. At the end of Goubrine One a black column of smoke was rising fast and opening out like a flower. A tug had hit another plane as it was being fuelled and both had blown up. The smell of burning fuel and rubber caught in my throat like the smell of fear and I hurried back to my tent. Then Smith put his head round the flap to tell me it was time to go.

19.   Waterloo Bridge

So now you understand how I came to be in the Horsa glider that landed heavily in the field near Waterloo Bridge that Hoppy had pointed out to Chatterton on the aerial photos, and that Chatterton had been so unhappy about. Without any brakes to slow it down my glider moved rapidly through the field towards the canal bank two hundred feet away. At the controls next to me Dougie Hatton was hauling on the brake lever for all his life was worth. When the Horsa's nose hit the canal bank the metal bolts binding the floor of the cockpit to the rest of the glider sheared and the nose tilted up. Dougie's body slammed against his restraining belt but I wasn't strapped in and I shot through the hole in the canopy that Charlie Coombs had made, over the canal bank and into the water just as the glider exploded behind me.

For a few seconds I flailed around in terror but before I could tear off my heavy kit, I felt the muddy bottom with my feet. I climbed the other bank of the canal and rolled down into a bed of thistles. Patting my body all over I concluded I wasn't injured but I couldn't remember anything that had happened to me after I had stepped into the Horsa's cockpit. All that came back to me later. Peace enfolded me as though I was held in the palm of a giant protecting hand and I slept. When I awoke I noticed an orange glow at one side of the sky. The warmth I had felt while I lay in the patch of thistles had faded away and the knot of fear in my belly was back. I rubbed the scar on my temple. We must be bombing Syracuse, I decided. That meant it was after oh-two-thirty-hours. How was the attack on Waterloo Bridge going? Where on earth was the glider with sergeant Smith and my platoon?

Standing up I felt all over again for wounds. Shapes of olive trees loomed through the darkness and I remembered that I had been swimming, so I crawled up the bank of the canal. The glow of the burning city was reflected in the water but I couldn't spot my glider. I crouched and splashed canal water over my face before following the line of the canal towards the fires. As I stumbled along I took the revolver out of its holster. The Allied planes had turned for home but guns were firing somewhere in the distance. Above my head the constellations were clearly visible and I glimpsed the brief line made by a shooting star as it fell. The air was warm and I could see the outlines of the trees and smell the scent of summer fruits, lemons and oranges and peaches. Branches brushed against my face and parched grass crackled under my boots. I noticed that near the canal the air was humid and there was a slight mist over the ground. How different this lushness, the scents, the trees, the slight dampness in the night air, was compared to Africa, I mused.

After a while I halted because I was nervous about the noise I was making. Around me I could hear the rustling of leaves on the lemon trees and then the snap of a twig. I wondered what animals were about. Did the Sicilians have badgers or foxes? An owl hooted somewhere in front of me and I heard a fox's bark. I started walking again. Close at hand came a loud sound as a bird flew off the tree where it had been resting. When I had walked beside the bank for about twenty minutes I heard the sound of firing ahead so I advanced very cautiously, dodging from tree to tree. Meanwhile the mist had begun to grow distinctly whiter and the dampness in the air was more noticeable. Objects - a wooden fence, a telephone pole with wires and a road - gradually emerged from the gloom. The shooting had ceased and voices were raised in excitement. Now I could see the grey concrete of the blockhouse on the bridge, the outlines of the eucalyptus trees on the other side and the orange trees nearby. Pieces of paper were scattered on the ground and the body of an Italian soldier with his pockets turned out was lying beside the next tree. I realised I had reached Waterloo Bridge and was in danger of being shot by my own side.

Hiding behind the tree I shouted out the password, waited for the response and walked up to the bridge. A lieutenant was talking to a couple of sergeants outside the nearest blockhouse. Other soldiers were crouching under the parapet with their guns beside them, smoking cigarettes or brewing up tea. With the coming of light the smells were more intense. The acrid sharp smell of the eucalyptus trees, the tang of oranges and whiffs of cordite mingled with the chemical smell of the blocks of paraffin which the soldiers were using to cook their breakfasts. They did not look up as I walked by. Submissive, they were simply glad to be alive when some of their comrades were dead, and they were awaiting orders.

My squaddies nowadays often ask me what the old British army was like. The soldiers I commanded, I tell them, fell into three types: the submissive soldier, the bullying soldier and the reckless soldier. The submissive type was common. Most conscripts were calmly submissive. Many enjoyed soldiering, the company of men, the open air life and big helpings of food. The bullying type was common among the corporals and sergeants. Those who were by nature sly men managed their bullying with some diplomacy. The diplomatic bullies cajoled and wheedled and got their orders obeyed by withholding or granting little favours – giving a favoured soldier a rest from cookhouse duties or putting a difficult soldier on point duty when patrolling. But for the most part bullies in the army were just plain bullies who used their authority as it suited them.

The rarest type of soldier was the reckless man, largely because in wartime he either stopped being reckless or got killed. Army instructors were good at spotting the reckless types; the joker, the man too stupid to understand danger; and the killer, the man who enjoyed danger and sought it out. The jokers were kept away from the front line. The vicious men were handled carefully so that all their hatred was turned against the enemy. Natural born killers are the most valuable men you can have fighting beside you, I tell my young friends. They had led the rush onto

Waterloo Bridge and four of them were dead.

The lieutenant was very young and exuded submissiveness as I approached. He was enormously pleased at having captured the bridge but he was worried that something would go wrong and was eager to hand over his responsibilities. 'Luckily we landed right by the bridge,' he said proudly, 'and took it at a rush. Only lost four men. We've put prisoners and wounded inside the blockhouse. Shall I tell you my casualties or can that wait until later?'

With a cold shock I realised that I was the senior officer. But the boy lieutenant seemed to have things in hand. The telephone lines and the cables to the demolition charges had been cut. He walked across the bridge with me. When we got to the second blockhouse he explained that the enemy pillbox between the bridge and the sea was still holding out and we should stay under cover. Where the parapet ended we ran forward to a roadside ditch. A sergeant and five men had a Bren trained up the road to Syracuse.

It was very quiet. We could see the fires on the other side of the harbour but there were no more explosions. An Italian soldier came down the road towards us on a bicycle. He climbed off the bicycle and presented a leave pass. It was beginning to look as though the defenders of Waterloo Bridge had not had time to telephone. I was about to run back to the further end of the bridge when the sergeant pointed out the headlamps of a vehicle. It was a large open touring car driving very fast. As it passed us the sergeant raked it with his Bren but it continued on up to the blockhouse and stopped. I ran towards the car. The driver's door was open and he had fallen onto the gravel. An older officer with gold braid on his epaulettes was shouting and waving his arms. One of the soldiers hit him in the stomach with the butt of his rifle and he gasped and sat down. This was a comic opera sort of warfare, I thought.

The driver's body was carried to the side of the road and the officer disappeared into the blockhouse. I looked back at the approach to the bridge. Three small armoured cars were approaching but as they neared the bridge they slowed and almost stopped, like hunting dogs sniffing for the scent. I jumped into the ditch beside the sergeant and the young lieutenant. Then the pillbox opened up and bullets spattered into the side of the parapet. At that noise the armoured cars jerked forward and we watched the first car rumble past. It halted as it reached the bridge and the wreck of the general's car. The other vehicles stopped as well and a soldier in the ditch stood up and rolled a grenade under the chassis of the middle car. Its wheels were lifted off the road by the blast. Fuel spilled onto the road and caught fire in a burning choking sheet of flame. The hatch door at the side opened and a man jumped out. His overalls were on fire. He stumbled towards where we crouched but fell heavily and the flames on the road licked over his body.

On the bridge the soldiers fired their rifles and the sergeant in the ditch sprayed the vehicles with bullets. The lead vehicle backed off the bridge and banged into the burning car. It was trying to push the car out of the way but instead came off the road itself and lodged in the ditch with its wheels spinning uselessly and its machine gun still firing. But the turret was jammed and the bullets hit the ground a few yards away. Reversing up the road the third car disappeared. The engine of the trapped vehicle roared and its gun spat flame but it was like a cockroach on its back with legs flailing. The sergeant crawled past me and lobbed a grenade. This one knocked against a wheel and when it exploded only the wheel came off. But the gun stopped firing and the hatch door opened slowly, almost tentatively. A hand waved a white handkerchief.

The men inside the pillbox carried on fighting and cost us a couple of men, but after we mortared them silence descended on Waterloo Bridge for a bit. We had won a victory of sorts, I realised and began to wonder when I would get the chance to tell Bella about it. Later again I remembered about looking for sergeant Smith and all my soldiers.

20.   The Ear

When Monty's troops from the beaches had passed through and taken the town, I didn't know what to do next. I couldn't discover anything about my men. The boy lieutenant was eager to leave but I kept him and his platoon awaiting orders. It was afternoon before a jeep stopped by the bridge and out stepped a small man dressed in the blue uniform of a captain in the Royal Marines that was far too large for him. The marine captain looked furious and kicked the blockhouse with his foot but then congratulated me on taking the bridge. It was general Hoppy. Lawrence was driving another jeep, looking pale. He broke into a huge smile when he saw me.

'You and Wright are in charge of prisoners,' barked out Hoppy before jumping back into his jeep. Lawrence stayed behind. He told me that there had been a plan for the prisoners too and it had gone wrong. I looked at him. He loved explaining things, even in the middle of a war zone.

'We're going to the quarries. One of Hoppy's bright young men read that the Syracusans imprisoned the defeated Greeks in the quarries at the edge of town,' he said. 'So he planned that Italian prisoners should be sent to the same place as the old Greeks. Prisoners are a nuisance but it's our job to see they're handled well. Hoppy remembers from the last war how many prisoners were shot and he wants to make sure nothing happens to spoil his public image.'

'But why am I in charge instead of somebody else? And what are you doing working for Hoppy?' I asked.

'We're all having to muck in. The bright young officer drowned in Hoppy's glider. Most of us did. Have you really no idea of what's happened, Dodo?"

The wind had done it, he told me that evening. At Goubrine the wind had whipped up the surface of the salt pan and crumpled the telex form in Lawrence's hand as he walked across to his operations hut. He opened the hut door and stepped out of the wind. He knew what failure was. It was the smell that had come into the hut with him, burning rubber and fuel from a crashed aircraft.

'The plan is to release six miles offshore,' said Chatty. 'If this telex about the offshore gale is still correct we should change that to two miles out or the gliders will all fall into the sea.'

'Sir, if we release two miles out the flak from the defences will put off the Dakotas. Don't forget that most of general Williams's pilots have no experience of enemy action. The operation is risky enough. We don't want to 'up the ante', if I can put it that way.'

'This isn't the moment for one of your Babu jokes, Loll.'

'Sorry. I suggest you split the difference and order the release four miles out. And keep the height at three thousand feet as agreed.'

'Agreed. You'd better get over to the glider and meet the general. I'll join you later.'

Seated inside the glider and putting on the Mae West lifejacket and harness, Lawrence saw that Hoppy's hands were shaking. He said he wanted help to recall the code for talking to the Americans. A different colour for each day: that was an improvement over the damned silly code they used in Algeria. Tomorrow was red and the day after was green and the day after that was blue, or was it purple? How did the bloody code run?

'Hoppy spent most of the flight talking non-stop to me. Rubbish, most of it, but there was one interesting story. At university he stole a complete German field gun. He said the watchman walked past three feet from his head as he lay beneath the gun, sawing it free from its trophy base. He felt the thrill of combat for the first time, the urge to take on the man if he noticed anything and club him into silence. A hundred students under his command pulled the gun out of Jesus through a gap sawn in the railings and through the middle of Cambridge. He had men with sticks on patrol ahead to scare off any night policeman. By the time his college clock tolled midnight, he said, the gun sat silent and massive in front of the Master's lodgings. And do you know what he was most proud of in the whole thing?'

'No.'

'That they did it in sub-fusc, wearing mortarboards, gowns and white ties. He's completely mad, you know. Let's get to the quarries. Hop in.'

Sometimes at the Gate we get young people stepping off the trains in the midst of all the old folks, dressed in grubby civilian clothes with rucksacks on their backs. Their bus has overturned somewhere in the Andes or a ferry has gone down in the Indian ocean, and before they realise what's happened to them they're sitting on the Tube pulling into our platform. They remind me of the Italian prisoners I had to look after for the next couple of days. Most of them were no more than boys. Past the railway station and up the hill to the quarries we shepherded a couple of hundred teenagers late that afternoon. The officers stood out among them with their upright bearing. Lawrence and I buzzed from one end of the column to the other in his jeep and the lieutenant provided the foot guards. Inside the quarries we hurried them past the neat wooden benches overhung by branches of tangerine trees with young green fruit and sent them to a grotto cut out of the soft rock. It was called the Ear.

Pink and white bands of stone like a layer cake formed the high walls next to the Ear. Nothing grew between the stones at the top where the sun beat down, but from cracks in the lower part of the walls hung ferns the length of a man's body. At the bottom of the quarry the walls were stained brown by damp. From the path the Ear looked to me like a tall thin arch from a gothic cathedral that a giant had taken up and twisted between his finger and thumb. The first prisoners halted where the light grew dim and the column backed up until the guards at the front shouted at the guards at the rear. Then I led all the prisoners into the gloom of the cave like a shepherd with his sheep. Even right at the back, two hundred feet from the entrance where you couldn't see the daylight at all, it was still high and narrow. Pigeons flew cooing in and out of their nests near the roof.

For a few minutes our human sheep milled around nervously, treading on one another's feet while the guards watched at the entrance with rifles and bayonets. The more alert ones bagged places where they could sit with their backs resting against the walls. Others stretched out on the sandy floor and went to sleep. Men pissed against the wall but when one man lowered his trousers and began to shit I slapped him and he fell over with his pants round his ankles. Then the Italian officers and I made the other prisoners clear a space near the entrance as a latrine and they wiped their hands afterwards on the walls.

We had no food to hand out and Lawrence went off to find some water. The prisoners ate what they had on them. Those without went hungry. Water bottles were passed around although that was near an end when Lawrence returned with a water cart. The night deepened and the chattering died away. I patrolled from one end of the Ear to the other. At the back I found I could hear the noises made by the guards outside – not just their talk but the sounds they made as they spat or grounded their rifles. I even heard the scratch of match against rock as cigarettes were lighted. The Ear transmitted every sound so you could whisper a phrase at the entrance and somebody at the back would hear it perfectly. Lovers could come here to whisper endearments to each other. I dreamed about proposing marriage to Bella.

The lieutenant's men cooked up supper of corned beef and potatoes with their paraffin blocks and Lawrence told us about Hoppy and his glider. He tried to make it sound amusing but his jokes fell very flat. We had all seen too much death that day to find any comedy in it. As their glider neared the island Lawrence could see the bursts of flak ahead through the Perspex canopy of the cockpit. The Dakota tug climbed steeply to get to the correct height for releasing the glider. Lawrence heard Chatty in the cockpit shouting to the pilot that it was too early to release. Suddenly flak exploded close to the Horsa and the tug turned and dived away. The glider was pulled down after it.

The pilot shouted in a horrified voice that the Yanks were pushing off. Chatty hit the release lever and the glider lost height and headed towards the surface of the sea. With a bang it smashed into the water and started to sink. Somebody got the hatch open but only a few inside managed to unbuckle their safety harnesses and swim out before the fuselage filled with water and disappeared. Men were struggling to get rid of their heavy kit and inflate their Mae Wests. Lawrence had to fight hard to stay clear of a drowning man who was clawing out for somebody to hold on to. Otherwise he would have gone to the bottom as well. The lucky ones included Hoppy and Chatty and they lay in the water and watched the flak and tracer in the night sky above. Once bombs fell all around and an aircraft hit the sea not far away. The burning fuel from its tanks crept along the waves towards them.

At dawn a British destroyer that was collecting the crews of ditched gliders steamed slowly by and an hour later Lawrence and Chatty stood on the deck of the destroyer looking at Hoppy, who was striding up and down in wet clothes with his hands clasped behind his back. Bofors guns fired at the German dive-bombers overhead and pieces of hot metal pattered onto the deck near his feet but he paid them no attention. Lawrence knew Hoppy wanted to get ashore and into action, to lose his fury at the Yanks in the middle of combat.

A dapper naval captain came up to them and gazed at Hoppy with a smile on his lean face. He coughed politely until the general in his soaking uniform turned around.

'It is Hopkinson, isn't it?' he said. 'What a lark seeing you again. Come and have breakfast and I'll fix up some dry clothing. Our Marines are bound to have something vaguely military that you can try on. Haven't seen you since '22 when I rowed in the Jesus boat. That was just after you'd taken our gun, if you remember.'

Hoppy glared past the captain at Lawrence, and Lawrence said he had to pretend he hadn't heard anything.

We were finishing the bully beef when the lieutenant came back and said he had found somewhere for us to sleep. It was the villa of the director who had run the excavations. Inside we found the place a complete mess. Somebody had shot the lock off the wall safe and books were scattered over the floor. I had to stop the soldiers taking a big old book with them for lavatory paper. You never know, I thought, turning over its leaves and trying to make sense of the old-fashioned writing, it might be quite important. Marshal Foch would know. I went to sleep that night thinking of Bella.

21.   Bella's diary

July 12th.

The time is three in the morning and I am sitting at the pharmacy counter. The hospital is very quiet. We arrived here at Syracuse yesterday. It already seems a long time. So much has happened, including just a few minutes ago, and I have to pinch myself to realize I have been in Europe for less than a day. I was already on deck when my first Sicilian dawn broke. The destroyer left Bizerta the evening before and I stayed up all night drinking the sailors' cocoa. At dawn I saw the low shape of the island looking like a thick smear of mascara on the horizon. The invasion fleet was moored in a huge bay. Above the ships barrage balloons bobbed to and fro. They were giving protection against dive bombers, a sailor said, and he pointed out to me the fighter aircraft that glinted high overhead. The warships were patrolling up and down like watchdogs. He pointed out how the little landing craft were being filled with supplies from the cargo vessels. Their black metal cranes swung to and fro as they emptied the holds of equipment. I suppose it comes all the way from London.

A kind officer with a beard lent me his binoculars so I could see the men and vehicles moving around on the long white beaches of the bay. As each landing craft dropped its gate onto the sand, a gang of men moved in to unload the stores into trucks that waited their turn. War is such a strange thing, not at all what I expected. I couldn't feel any sense of danger. When I compare it to the few German trucks that came to our own town square I wonder how can anything stand against what the English are doing? Beyond the beaches the land rises gradually, with bright green groves and the lighter silvery hue of olive trees. It reminds me of the hills behind my town in Africa. From time to time there was a small puff of smoke below the crest of the hills. Whether it was the ships firing or artillery on shore I don't know. I can't believe the enemy can fight back against all this.

We sailed on to Syracuse past the old castle at the point and dropped anchor in the big harbour. I've never seen a city before. From the fort at one end to the docks at the other smoke rose above the white buildings in a thin shimmering stream. The city has been bombed again by the Luftwaffe and the enemy are trying to prevent us unloading supplies. On the shore men were working hard. The officer told me they were clearing the docks of debris and booby traps. The bulldozers on the mole pushed the debris around and this produced a low haze of dust. As I watched it eddied offshore and dropped slowly towards the surface of the harbour. Further round the bay a tanker lies on its side, half on the sand and half in the water. You can smell the burning fuel but the sea around the destroyer was wonderfully clear.

I bent over the gangrail and looked into the depths of the water, light blue near the surface but a deeper hue further down. Schools of small fish darted about as though trying to shake off an enemy. These fish swim like the boys in my town ride their bicycles, I thought. But further off in the water I could see the large dark shape of the wing of a plane and I turned my eyes away. As we entered the harbour I had seen the wrecks of the gliders. They must have broken up as they hit the surface, because there were fuselages and wings and tail planes lying on the bottom on their own. I hope all the men escaped before they sank but I saw a few bodies bobbing about. I do hope Dodo is fine!

At the quayside they put us into trucks for the short drive to the hospital. Not all the damage from the night's air raid had been cleared away and our vehicles bumped slowly over the rubbish in the streets. We gazed at the townsfolk, who ignored us as they picked their way among the rubble. I am amazed at how thin and pinched their faces are. They look as though they haven't eaten well for months, while I had bacon and eggs for breakfast. On an impulse I tossed a handful of Bengal Lancers into the street. A woman in black bent down and put the cigarettes in her bag without looking at our truck, then walked quickly away.

'Why on earth did you do that?' asked Barbara who was sitting opposite.

'In Bizerta they fight for cigarettes and I wanted to see what happens.'

'But they're the enemy, stupid.'

Our hospital is on the waterfront next to the post office. Bombs have blown out the windows so the empty frames are boarded up. It was very busy there. Casualties from the fighting were overflowing from wards into the corridors, out of the building down the steps and into the piazza where they lay in the sunshine. As we climbed down from the trucks an ambulance came over the bridge from the mainland and busily unloaded. The stretcher bearers chattered comfortingly to the wounded men, I noticed. But when they were motioned away from the entrance, I could tell they lost interest and were just searching for somewhere to leave their burden while they went for a cup of tea. Surgical teams were at work moving from case to case. We were taking our things out when there was a crescendo of noise and a German fighter swept low over the square. For an instant its shadow passed over me and I felt scared.

Drugs for the patients come from the pharmacy here on the ground floor. Each wooden shelf has the Latin names of the drugs painted in gold lettering but the floor was covered with broken glass and the powdered remains of the drugs when we arrived. We brought plentiful supplies and cleared the shelves and laid them out. But the penicillin promised by professor Florey hasn't arrived and the doctors say all they can do is cover up the wounds to keep off the flies and stop any infection spreading. When I walked down the hallways carrying medicines to the wards this afternoon there was a sweet sickly smell in the air. Now I recognise the odour of gangrene from an infected wound.

This evening the matron told me to look after the pharmacy for the night. And that was how I had my big adventure! A strange doctor appeared about half an hour ago when the place was deserted. He walked through the door from the kitchen, and I thought that was a bit odd. He wore a white coat and carried a clipboard but he had an old-fashioned wooden stethoscope poking out of his pocket and he was dark-skinned, definitely not an Englishman. He began to talk to me in a slow Italian which I could barely understand until he put a small glass phial on the counter. I picked it up and looked at the label. It had contained morphine. He placed a gold chain alongside the phial and spreading out his fingers offered the chain to me in return for five ampoules of the morphine. He said he had been the chief doctor here at the hospital and he needed drugs for his patients who had been evacuated to make way for the English.

So I weighed the chain in my hand. Boxes of the drug are stacked under this counter. The nurses use Pentathol to knock out the wounded before the surgeons operate on them but they give morphine in the post-op wards. To be honest, the main job of the nurses here is only to keep wounds clean and give regular injections of morphine. The wounded become calm and dreamy and some even hum bits of tunes. So we have lots of morphine. I reached down and handed the ampoules to the funny-looking doctor. He wrapped them in his handkerchief and raised my hand to his mouth to kiss it. I have just looked again at the gold chain under the light of the lamp. It is a lovely thing, very old I think. Now I need to decide where to hide it, and then just make an amendment in the book listing the pharmacy's stocks: one little stroke of the pencil and the matter is settled. The nurses do it all the time when they break a bottle or something goes missing, so why shouldn't I? I have to take what chance offers, after all, and this is a wonderful start to my new life in Europe.

22.   Primosole

Sicily was as tough as anything I saw in the desert. The Germans fought hard to stop us crossing each river. Three days after we took Waterloo Bridge I was lying in the long brown grass and looking through binoculars at the massive flattened cone of Etna. They had found the remains of my glider and my platoon. So as an officer without troops I was condemned to do odd jobs for general Hoppy. The previous morning we had been summoned down to the quayside at Syracuse. Montgomery sat with his maps spread out on a café table and told Hoppy in his prim schoolmaster's voice about Primosole Bridge and how it must be taken for the advance to continue. I knew that Hoppy was painfully aware that he must organise this second attack better than the first, but he did not know how.

'I'll give you some artillery support,' Monty promised and I was on this hillside to make sure that it happened.

The shape of the mountain in front reminded me of the straw dish covers that the native servants used to put over the food at Pindi to stop the flies. Although Etna was thirty miles away I felt I could almost reach out and lift it up as I would lift the dish covers in the mess to get at the curry underneath. The road along which our truck had come crossed the ridge to the right and wound down towards the flat plain that lay between us and the volcano. On the plain itself was the Simeto river, curling lazily towards the sea. The coastal road crossed it by the long Primosole bridge. Beyond the bridge was the German aerodrome at Catania with its anti-aircraft guns. Down there were orange and lemon groves, good cover for the Germans on the other side of the bridge.

The artillery spotters I had brought up from Syracuse put down the heavy wireless sets under the shade of a cork tree and started to dig a slit trench in the hard soil but gave up after a few minutes. Setting up the range-finders the crew called in their co-ordinates. They were fresh off the boat from England. Soon it was fully dark. Liberators bombed Catania aerodrome again and on the plain the thin lights of tracer bullets and the occasional flare showed us where the British commandos were holding onto one end of the bridge, waiting for the boys in the gliders to reinforce them. Through the hot night air came the sound of tugs like the whine of mosquitoes and enemy searchlights flashed into life. The spotting team worked steadily to give the positions of the guns as tracer came up from the other side of the bridge at the tug aircraft. Small fires were burning where incendiary bullets had set fire to the grass.

A tug flew over our heads and as I looked up I saw the distinctive shape of a twin-engined Albemarle. There was only one Albemarle in the force so that had to be Peter up there, towing a Horsa. The flak was worse than at Syracuse but the plane flew straight towards the drop zone. The glider cast off and went down steeply into the inferno of tracer and fires. Peter's plane turned to escape but a Dakota with an engine on fire was coming straight towards him. The Albemarle wrenched to one side and the wingtips missed each other by inches, but he had lost height and was heading back into the flak. As I watched two shells exploded near the plane. They tore a hole in the starboard wing, the engine feathered and stopped, and the plane slipped sideways in a shallow dive.

From the hillside I kept track of the Albemarle which was flying towards the distant black shape of Etna with an engine on fire. Peter had fought it back to an even keel and it was too low for the guns but a searchlight like a jeering finger followed his course. Overhead another Dakota was engulfed in flame from the fuel spilling from its unprotected tanks. It spiralled down towards the hillside where I lay and I thought it was sure to hit me. When the plane was no more than a few hundred feet above the ground it exploded like a rocket on Guy Fawkes' night. Drops of burning fuel spattered onto my clothes and I jumped wildly, beating them out with my hands.

When I recovered from my fright I realised the anti-aircraft fire had almost stopped. Far away I could see the sparks from the wounded Albemarle. Peter had gained height and I thought he must soon turn out over the sea and run for Africa and safety. But the plane was heading straight towards the volcano. I watched in dumb horror and after a while a flame blossomed on the dark flank of Etna like a child lighting a match and blowing it out. Now, I thought, there's only Lawrence and me.

I drove back in the light through a succession of ruined villages, keeping well away from the crowded main road. The sun was well up when I halted the truck by a grove of olive trees. The men brewed tea in the thin shade and ate their rations. I was too shaken to try to get them to mount guard.

'We'll rest here until it gets a bit cooler and then go down to the main road. Hopefully the jams will have cleared.'

The men were stretched out under the trees and they regarded me with grins on their faces as I walked back to the truck and lay beneath it – an old Desert Rats precaution. What happened next I can only guess at. An escape party, some collection of assorted German infantrymen, drivers, orderlies, cooks and clerks, must have come across us on their retreat and been amazed that the Tommies had put out no sentries. Perhaps the team which had been lugging the heavy mortar disagreed with the officer's decision to skirt quietly around because they saw a chance to use up the ammo on us and dump the mortar. Maybe all they wanted was our rations and cigarettes. I don't know. All I remember is waking to the sound of the mortar rounds exploding among the olive trees and the crackle of machine-gun fire. Then after a silence I heard the regular snap of a pistol shot as the officer went round finishing off our wounded. The Germans climbed into the truck and took whatever they wanted. I lay underneath and waited for them to go away. Then my memory goes blank. Probably the Germans blew up the vehicle as they left. And I don't know how or where I was found.

All I can say is that I came slowly awake in the back of a truck rattling along a road, feeling numb and with my pains located somewhere offshore of my sensations. I recognised the effects of a morphine shot. Gradually as I focused I could make out a man's voice. It was explaining his plans for after the war. Those harsh whisky-soaked tones had to belong to Scuffy Lintle, I thought. I tried to open my eyes and get up. I couldn't move or speak but with one eye I could see him. He was sitting on a coffin. The back of the truck seemed to be full of them. Scuffy was talking nineteen to the dozen.

'When I get back to Blighty, which I don't intend to do mind you, I'll explore the whole island the way it's never been explored before. I'm going to find the highest spot in each county and just look out over all the blessed landscape and watch the clouds fly by.'

'That would be grand in the Trossachs,' agreed a Scots voice. 'But the highest point in Norfolk is just a pimple.'

'You sweaty socks don't know anything. The highest point in Norfolk is Beacon Hill, and it's 336 feet high.'

'How d'ye know that?'

'My pater was the padre at Burnham Market just nearby. As a lad I used to walk to the top. There was a beech tree and I would climb up into it as high as I could go and look south, straining to see the tropics where adventure lay. Boyhood of Drake, really.'

'Raleigh. Ye mean the boyhood of Raleigh.'

'Mind you, I'll do all my climbing in winter when the hills aren't as steep.'

'How's that?'

'When it rains in the winter the ground at the bottom of the hill soaks up all the water that runs down. So it swells up and rises and it's less distance to walk up the hill. Hold on a minute, I think he's coming round.'

'I'll give him another shot of Omnipon, shall I?'

'Don't waste it, Hamish. It's only his leg. And his face is a bit of a mess too. Oh all right if you insist.'

'He's a lucky lad. Suppose I'll have to drive up there again and bring in the others?'

'That's our job, sergeant. And tell Madass to order some more wooden boxes while you're at it.'

I felt the prick of a needle and suppose I must have passed out again for I remember nothing more.

23.   Bella's diary

July 14th

The most amazing thing has happened. Dodo has come back. This morning I helped unload a wounded man . The pile of coffins inside the truck made me gasp. I covered my mouth and asked, 'But do you have his identity tag? It's been burned off and we don't have a name.' The man in charge looked like an ogre with the strings hanging down from his hat and the patch over his eye. I cringed when this horrible man patted me on the shoulder. He actually laughed as he said: 'His name is T F Bundy, dear girl. Get the matron to put that down.'

When I told the sister she laughed as well. She said it was an old hospital joke, medical humour, like putting a black spot on the patient's sheet. I suppose I looked blank for she said: 'Doesn't make any sense unless you've read 'Treasure Island', which you haven't done, not being English.'

She went on to say that TF Bundy stood for: 'Totally Fucked But Unfortunately Not Dead Yet.' So the ogre was only playing his tricks on me.

I went for supper where I listened to the other nurses talk. Something about the new arrival nagged at the back of my mind. Across the table that wicked bitch Barbara was describing a patient and her friend said, 'What about that man with the burns in Alamein ward? He's recovering and only yesterday I stopped that prick Poticare from giving him the black spot. Poticare said he was as dead as a dodo.'

I screamed and jumped to my feet. Barbara's friend looked at me in astonishment.

'Did I say something?' she asked.

'You mentioned dodos, darling,' replied Barbara. She called after me as I ran from the table: 'They're probably a forbidden meat in whatever part of Africa the girl comes from!'

In the ward I leaned over this dearest TF Bundy of mine and touched the mark made by the cricket ball on his temple. Since then Dodo's bed has been moved to the ward for officers only. His kit has just arrived, including the little statuette that Papa gave him. He hasn't properly woken up yet.

July 15th

Dodo's boss paid a visit. He strode into the ward with a thin man in glasses running after him and came up to where I was sitting by the bed. But he didn't recognise me from that dinner in Tabarka last week. He seized Dodo's patient record and turned the pages rapidly.

'I see you're being looked after in a first-class way, Deeds. Congratulations sister,' he said, beaming at me.

'I can tell you confidentially that I have put you in for an MC,' the general said, leaning over the bed. 'It's important that our success with gliders is recognised. There has been some shamefully defeatist talk. Bags of hard fighting ahead in Italy. Look forward to seeing you fit and well soon. Did you say something?' He gazed deeply into Dodo's face, and then he turned to the man in glasses.

'Always important to visit the casualties, Loll. Sometimes I feel that the Lord has given me the ability to heal men. Or at any rate the power to pass over my own confidence and will to win. '

And then he was gone. But a few minutes later the other man returned in a great hurry, glancing over his shoulder. He took Dodo's hand very gently in his own and I think Dodo recognised him because he smiled and tried to say something. The other man leaned over him and kissed his forehead before turning to me and asking how quickly I thought Dodo would be better. I replied that it would only be a few more days, according to sister.

'I must try to keep him away from the general.' he said. 'The man is simply the angel of death.'

July 19th

Dodo will be discharged tomorrow. He started walking as soon as he could but it seems to me his limp is a bit worse than before. He doesn't want to go home, he says, now that he has found me again. The nice man in specs is an old friend and has arranged for him to be transferred to the staff of the new military governor. Somebody needs to be in charge of dealing with the booby traps that the Germans have left behind. I hate this idea but Dodo says it means we can go out together in the evenings sometimes and have picnics at weekends.

Later

The strange doctor came again last night when I was on duty at the pharmacy. I have given him some more morphine and he gave me an old brooch, a lovely thing.

July 22nd.

The evening was a lovely temperature. Dodo walked me up to the old Greek theatre by the quarries and made me climb onto the stage while he sat in the audience with his bad leg stuck out in front of him. I recited a speech by Racine that they made us learn at school and standing behind Dodo some soldiers clapped, but I don't believe they understood a word. I curtsied and took his hand as I stepped down. I am glad that he has come back. I believe it is what I wanted. But I have to confess that he is a bit disappointing. He doesn't have a lot to say except that he loves me. It's a bit boring and I have to find lots of different ways to avoid saying that I love him too. Because I don't. I have developed a lot since coming to Europe. I own some beautiful things now and I don't believe he would approve.

July 23rd

The doctor is coming every night now. I am worried about how much morphine I am stealing.

Part Two: Enemies

Something was in the air, something subtle and strange, an intolerable atmosphere like a public smell – the smell of the invasion. It filled our houses and streets, changed the taste of the food we ate and made us feel as though we had journeyed far away to a land of wild and dangerous tribes.

  – Guy de Maupassant

1.   November 1963

Bless me father for I have sinned. I can't recall how long it is since my last confession. These are my sins. I don't know where to begin. Sit closer to me and let me drink from that glass of water on the bedside table. No, taste it yourself first. Wait a minute. How does it taste? Do you feel all right? Then let me drink some. You can't be too careful, even here in the prison hospital. Only a fortnight ago they poisoned one of the patients in the other ward. He drank a cup of coffee from the urn they bring around each morning and was dead in half an hour. It was strychnine, they tell me. Once a man in the condemned cells here was poisoned. He was due to be hanged the next morning. Why in the condemned cell itself, you ask? Just to show they could. Nobody can escape them, that's the message they want everybody to hear. What about the President of America they've just murdered in Texas? A clever business, that. They killed the man who killed the President as well so there was nobody left to talk.

You know the joke, father, about the man who tells his son that Einstein is dead? Why is he dead? the boy asks. Because he knew too much, the man replies. Me, I know too much. I don't have a chance. Either this lung cancer will kill me or they'll put me back in the jail and I'll be poisoned with my own dose of strychnine. A man has to eat and drink and you can't be lucky forever. I've been loyal, I've done my duty but now I'm in prison and they don't trust me to keep my trap shut. So why should I keep my mouth shut, especially to you, father? For twenty years I was Macaroni's right hand man. I protected him and killed his enemies. Don't be shocked. That's not the name he uses now, but when we first met in Syracuse the Tommies called him that as a joke. He was an anti-fascist in those days. All the Mafia were. Mussolini had hunted the Mafia down on the island and Mori worked for Mussolini.

Mori was my boss when I was a young policeman. Yes, that's right, I used to be a cop. It's going to be difficult to tell you what I have to confess. It's a murder, my first murder. I need time to get around to it and I want to start by telling you about the first time I shot a man, on a snowy afternoon forty years back. I did it to save Mori's life. The man I killed was a Mafia boss. He was old-style Mafia, before all the drugs came in. That was the fault of the Tommies and the Amis too. But let me stick to my story. I used to remember the day of the week and the date of my first kill but I am old now. I can recall how cold it was that morning before dawn, though.

I had been sleeping on a chair in the hotel corridor with the Winchester repeating rifle between my knees. I awoke with a start and grabbed the rifle. The bedroom door had opened and the girl slipped back out into the corridor. Her head was covered with a patterned shawl and she was barefoot. The girl stopped to put on her slippers, then she went down the stairs to the hotel lobby. It was still dark but I could see a glimmer of light under the bedroom door. I shivered and pulled the blanket tighter about me. I could hear Mori inside moving around. After a few minutes the girl came back. She was carrying a tray with a pot of coffee and some bread with jam made from figs. The coffee steamed in the chill air of the corridor. I motioned for her to halt and knocked on the door. The girl tried to push past and enter the room but the man took the tray and shut the door.

It was still dark when he came out of the bedroom and handed me coffee and the rest of the bread for my own breakfast. For safety's sake I went down the stairs in front of him. The lobby of the hotel was lit by oil lamps and I could see that outside the groom had brought the horses round. Mori nodded his big head at the manager behind the desk as he walked out. He was dressed for riding: long polished brown boots and a short leather jacket. On his head was a flat English riding cap. He was a big man.

'A morning ride to clear the head,' he said to the manager.

Outside the groom held the horses' heads. We bowed in the direction of the church on the other side of the square and crossed ourselves. Mori was still holding a piece of bread and he crumpled it in his hand and threw it to the birds hopping about before the statue in the centre of the square. He looked around the deserted square that was dusted with snow and across at the little café where two or three heads were turned towards us from the open door. Then he laughed.

'It has been snowing,' he said in his booming voice. 'We will have a splendid ride down at the lake.'

He crossed himself again and mounted. I passed him a thick woollen blanket that he arranged over his shoulders. The hooves of the horses clattered across the cobbles and we turned and headed steeply down the hill. Shreds of fog hung around the streets and it was beginning to get light. We passed the gate that led through the old walls and descended the twisting road past the Spanish fort and the temple. To one side of the road there were holes scraped out of the rock where the poorest people lived in those days. Wisps of smoke came from under the sacking that covered the entrances. Men coughed and spat dirty phlegm onto the grey stone and stared at us as we went down the hill towards the lake.

At the bottom of the hill we turned off the road onto an avenue of beech trees. The lake lay in front of us, shrouded in mist. Mori's horse broke suddenly into a gallop and I twisted in the saddle and looked into the oleander bushes on either side of the track, but there was nothing and I spurred after him. Have you ever been to that place, father? The lake is circular and about a mile across. Mussolini built a racetrack around it. On the other side we stopped the horses and dismounted in a wide clearing. The horses' breath steamed in the sodden air. Mori lit a cigarette and waved his gloved hand at the town above us. It rose in waves steeply from the green trees surrounding the lake. The temple was on one hill and the new town on another, separated by the cleft in the rock down which we had ridden. The buildings were of grey stone or painted over in colours of sienna and burnt ochre, and the roofs were covered in red and grey tiles.

'Impossible to take this town by force,' he said as I handed him the bandolier from his saddlebag. 'It has never been done in two thousand years. When the Moslems came...'

He buckled the bandolier around his waist.

'They had to bribe the garrison to surrender. Same with the Normans. It has always been the last town in Sicily to give in to the invaders. Win it with money if you can, for you can't win it by force of arms. The Duce has changed the name back to Enna but I prefer the old name. Castrogiovanni...,' he pronounced in his deep flat northern voice and threw the stub of the cigarette into the reeds that bordered the lake.

Slowly unbuttoning his coat he lifted off the short blackjack covered in leather from around his neck and hooked it onto the bandolier so that it hung down between his legs. I passed him the second Winchester in its oilskin and he unwrapped it and checked the action.

'This lake - Pergusa - is full of stories,' he said to me as he filled his rifle with shells from the saddlebag. 'Do you know them?'

'I am from Syracuse as your honour is aware and have no family in this country.'

'It was on this spot that the daughter of Ceres, whose temple you can see up there on the hill, was stolen and raped by Pluto.' He put the remaining cartridges into his jacket pockets.

'Pluto took her in his chariot under the lake to his palace in Hell. When her mother could not find her she cursed the world and gave us winter in revenge. Quite a story.'

He sighted over the surface of the lake with the Winchester.

I felt that my boss expected me to respond and I said, 'If your honour and I had lived in those days she could have appealed to us and we would have tracked down the criminal. The brute would have left tracks by the lakeshore for certain. We could have found out where he loaded the girl into his chariot because the marks would have been deeper in the mud.'

'Excellent point. I am making a good hunter out of you, young Carlo.'

'I would have gone willingly with your honour into hell to bring the poor girl back to her family. Then her mother would not have had the vendetta on all mankind and we wouldn't be standing about here in this wretched cold. It is starting to snow again.'

He traversed his rifle across the lake as though sighting on a god who had come like lightning from Etna to look for a pretty wife.

'But what would have happened if when we got down to Hell the victim denied she had been raped and said she was very happy with her new husband?'

'Now your honour is telling me a truly Sicilian story. My own grandfather took his wife by force after her father said he would not let her marry a poor fisherman. And my grandmother went with him not unwillingly. What could my great-grandfather do?'

I paused before going on and looked around again, for I was uncomfortable with the delay which meant more danger.

'My great-grandfather yearned with all his soul to stick a lupara into my grandfather's guts for dishonouring his daughter. But he couldn't because my grandfather was happy to take her to the altar. She was going to have his baby after all, so he knew she was a fertile woman who would give him a son. And who else would have her after that? It was the way things happened in those days.'

'So we would still have been left with the winter. Here are the others now!'

Two horses carrying policemen in their blue coats and peaked caps came trotting towards us out of the drifting mist of snow. Mori handed the rifle to me and swung into the saddle. He took off his flat cap and put on a big soft peasant's cap with a long peak which he pulled down over his face. I gave him back the blanket and rifle. Without a word he placed the rifle across his knees and kicked his heels into the horse's sides and made towards the other men. They parted to let him through and followed him. I brought up the rear with my Winchester lying across the saddle, glancing behind from time to time.

As long as we had the town in view we went south along mule trails. After half an hour we turned east and then north towards the Madonie mountains, riding fast but carefully. The sky cleared and the sun came up, and on our right we could see the vast cone of Etna sloping up to a flat top ringed with snow. We crossed the single track railway line and picked up the dirt road to Portella Crete and Villadoro. At Villadoro we left Mori in the street while I went into the bar with the other two to buy a cup of coffee and tell the owner we were taking a police captain from Rome to the station at Troina.

'It isn't fit to be out on the roads today,' said one, leaning across the counter, 'but these big-shot Fascists from the mainland want to show their balls.'

The other policeman joined in, drawing a hand across his neck in a cutting motion.

'I hope the bastard falls into a snowdrift and breaks his neck.'

They knew I was watching in case they told the barman what was going on. You never knew whom to trust in the days we were fighting the Mafia. They had their friends amongst the policemen then as well as now.

We took the Troina road out of the village and doubled back between fields where the winter wheat was struggling to poke through the snow. The route headed north through a land of eroded gullies into the Madonie where the hills rose towards sharp crests like fangs and there were small woods of beech and scrub-oak. Dead thistles lay by the sides of the path. It was an old pilgrim route over the mountains and we passed a metal shrine with a glass of red wine and a candle burning inside a jam jar by the little statue. Snow was falling again.

The snow is a gift from Our Lady, I thought. Oh, it shows up our tracks all right, but it will keep the bandits in their lairs today. And no shepherd will be out with his flock on the mountains in this weather. That means no tale-telling back to the town. Those murdering villains will be in their beds this morning with their whores beside them and a plate of spaghetti cooking in the kitchen. The snow is a blessing.

Our track took us past farmhouses in groves of eucalyptus trees where the corrugated iron roofs of the lean-tos were held down by stones against the wind. Once a woman came to the door but when she saw the four horsemen with their rifles she ducked back inside. Otherwise we saw nobody. The snow stopped at mid-morning and we halted at a little stream and rested the horses where the water ran clear from one shelf of rock to the other. On the other side of the stream we lost the track and pushed the horses uphill through thick tall grass. The hill town of Gangi came clearly into view. We had seen it early in the morning in the distance, peeping over the top of a hill like a rock outcrop or a piece of snow. Now it became an entire steep hillside of tiled roofs with patches of snow on them. The air was still and smoke rose from the chimneys.

Mori took out a pair of binoculars. 'I can see our boys down at the church,' he called. Then, putting them back: 'The silence is good. Let's keep it that way – no shooting until we have to. With any luck the place is completely sealed off.'

The pilgrim road we had been following ended at the Church of the Spirito Santo at the bottom of the town. In the courtyard of the sanctuary rifles were piled in stacks and policemen in blue and soldiers in field grey uniforms were stamping their feet to keep warm. The Fiat trucks were parked by the side of the road and men were standing in line to get hot coffee. A young captain came up to us. The big man stretched in the stirrups. 'Let's go in,' he cried and without looking around started up the cobbled hill past the church. The captain shouted at the men and they ran to the trucks. A mug of coffee spilled on the pavement. I followed my boss, spurring my horse to catch up. The streets were empty. On either side were low tunnels that gave entry to dark courtyards. Behind us the Fiat trucks were grinding up in low gear. Twisting around I saw that at each corner of the road a truck stopped to let off some troops.

Near the top of the town we emerged onto a wide terrace that looked down on the red-tiled roofs that overlapped one another like the scales of a mullet. The troops got out of the trucks and lined up between the church and a little baroque town hall. On the wall of the church was a large piece of white marble. It gave all the measurements used at Gangi market in the old Sicilian scale and in the metric scale introduced by the State. The old measure of length was the span of a man's hand, carved on the marble. Mori stretched his own big hand over the marble outline of the hand, covering it easily. He smiled to me and turned to address the troops.

'Today we together will end the rule of the Mafia in this town,' he thundered. 'You have been given the list of names. Enter the houses and take them and their weapons. If any bandit has fled you will bring his animals and wife and children to me at the square. You are quartered here until further notice.'

He flung up his hand still holding the peasant's cap.

'I command you to eat their food and drink their wine. I command you to sleep in the beds of the bandits.' He paused and added, 'Alone, of course!'

There was laughter and some clapping.

'You are here on an honourable and sacred task for our beloved Italy. Long live Italy!'

Later he sat in the weak sunlight on a bench in the middle of the square and quietly ate his lunch. I didn't eat but walked up and down with my rifle. Suddenly there was a movement at the top end of the terrace. By the side of a stone lion crouched above a pool of green water a group of men was standing. The shotguns were pointing at me and at Mori chewing his bread and salami. A very old man with a huge white beard stained with tobacco stepped forward.

'You are Prefect Mori?'

He got up, swallowed the bread and wiped the crumbs off his face with his hand.

'Yes, I am Mori,' he said, and he walked straight towards the old man who was pointing the shotgun at his belly. When he was a few feet away he stopped and stretched out his hand for the gun.

I knew what he was doing. He was shielding me from the men who were now all staring at him. I slowly moved my gun up and waited for him to get out of the way so I could let the rest of them have it. In the silence I held my breath and waited to see whether the old man would fire first. Then Mori threw himself down and I opened up. That was the first killing I ever did.

And the last? You know about that one, father. It's why I'm here in jail. Most were bad men, as bad as me if not worse. In the war I killed some Tommies. I don't feel comfortable about them, even though the English brought so much harm to our beloved island. I shot them on the night of the invasion.

2.   Cesare

The library sends round books in a cart so those of us in the hospital have some way of passing the time. I've never been a great reader but I have been doing some catching-up. Pass me that book on the table. It's an account of my city, Syracuse, written before the first world war. A thousand years ago, father, but I can just about remember it. Listen to this bit:

'During his summer cruise in the year 1909 the German Emperor paid a visit to the old island-city of Ortygia which is the heart of Syracuse. The imperial yacht with its three funnels shaped like upturned bells came into the grand harbour with its escorting cruiser. The next morning he insisted on standing upright as he was rowed ashore, nosing through the herd of little boats with painted eyes on each side of their bows. The local fishermen saw a man in early middle age with a clear expression and a fine bushy moustache, resplendent in a white admiral's uniform and gripping the gunwale. At the harbour steps the waiting dignitaries were pushed back by the Kaiser's guards who jumped out first to help him land and they escorted Wilhelm to the fountain of Arethusa where his sightseeing was to begin.

It took him only an hour to tour Ortygia, which is less than a mile long from end to end and a quarter of a mile wide. The island is shaped like an inverted thumbs-up sign, with the thumb pointing south into the Ionian sea. At the tip of the thumb is the Castello Maniace which guards the entrance to the grand harbour. Wilhelm landed at the base of the thumb and when he had admired the fountain and the mullet who swim in it he marched up the via Capodieci to where the church of San Benedetto stands like the first knuckle on the fist. Here the tall four-storied townhouses of the old aristocracy, with their jutting out Spanish balconies adorned with splendid flamboyant roses, face each other across the way like lines of pugilists spoiling for a fight.

The procession went on to the cathedral which towers above the surrounding buildings like a second knuckle and down the via Alagona to the piazza Archimede, the third knuckle of the island, and finally to the temple of Apollo at the base of the fist, where a delegation of worthies waited to present the town keys to the Kaiser. As the German sightseers strode by the citizens all wore their Sunday best and the main streets were bright with cotton bunting in the colours of royal Italy and imperial Germany.'

I saw the Kaiser. My father took me to see him come ashore. He had a withered arm, you know, and his sense of balance was terrible. He stumbled and fell when he landed. The glove that he held in his hand to disguise how short the arm was nearly dropped into the water. One of his guards placed it back between the Kaiser's fingers because he couldn't move the arm. But we cheered anyway. That was before all the wars began.

It is a maze of queer little back streets where I grew up off the via Alagona. I remember the women walking past my mother's window shrouded in black from head to foot and with huge bags of washing on their heads. She used to send me out for the macaroni that hung in strips above the entrance to the macaroni-shops. Each morning she bought our milk from a herd of goats from the countryside that the goatherd brought into the city. Our water came from water-barrels on a trolley drawn by a donkey and our bread from a little bakery on wheels that two boys pushed along the street, furnace and all.

In 1943 I was back in Syracuse, having been fired from the police because I had been too closely associated with Mori. Times were very hard for me. I was renting a room on via Picherale a hundred yards from where I was born and I had just been conscripted into the local militia that was supposed to be helping the army defend Syracuse.

Since the Kaiser's time things had changed: the water flowed from iron pipes and milk arrived in milk-churns. But the reason my childhood days came back to my mind on the evening I want to tell you about was that things had been going backwards for some weeks. Nobody had any milk to sell me and only that day the bombers had burned down the railway station and put the water plant out of commission.

Number 17 via Picherale isn't much changed. I was back there only a few months ago. It has a Gothic doorway with a broken griffon over the porch, an iron gallery on the first floor that stretches the width of the house, a stone staircase and the well in the courtyard. I had drawn up water to wash myself earlier from that well since the taps had run dry. The sun was beginning to set when I shut the house door and wheeled my bicycle past the church of Santa Maria towards the cathedral square with the mayor's offices. The refugees who had spent the night in the catacombs under the cathedral sat in groups on the ground on the shady side of the piazza. I turned into via Roma. Bombs had landed nearby and council workers in overalls and army caps were using long-handled shovels to move the rubble. They had a trailer with two wheels that attached to a motor bike.

'Hello Carlo!' shouted a worker and I responded as I walked on, watching the ground carefully for broken glass that might puncture the tyres of the bicycle. In the piazza Archimede a bomb had gone through the surface of the road and exploded in a cellar. Sailors in blue uniforms stood beside the crater and chatted. Across the piazza was a line of small shops. The tops and bottoms of the metal shutters covering their entrances had held firm but I noticed that the bomb blast had sucked the middles outwards and twisted them into strange shapes. The first shutter looked like half of a face with one black eye and its nose squashed up against the wall. I glanced past the shutter into the shop. Inside a pair of panties hung from the ceiling fan and brassieres and corsets covered the floor. The pedal of my bicycle caught on the strap of a silk slip and I bent down to untangle it. As I looked up a soldier who was guarding the shops to stop looting took his rifle off his shoulder. A young boy was coming out of the shop with an armful of lingerie. The soldier levelled the gun at him

'Do you want this for your sister back in Rome?' the boy shouted as he waved a bra in the soldier's face. 'I bet her tits aren't big enough. Why don't you all go home? We don't need you Italian bastards.'

The boy flung the clothing at the soldier's feet and turned to address me.

'We can fight on our own, can't we?' he asked.

The streets were clear of rubbish now and the rifle on my back banged against the mudguard as I cycled past the ruins of the temple of Apollo where on an ordinary day the buses would have been waiting to take peasants home from the Thursday market. I crossed the causeway connecting Ortygia to the new town. In both harbours to the east and west of the island ships were burning. The thick oil smoke from their bunkers drifted up into the cloudless July sky. On corso Umberto I halted opposite a modern block of flats and went inside. The door to the flat on the first floor was open and an old woman was ironing shirts in the hallway.

'Hello Carlo. Have you any news?'

'None, Flora, except that the English have bombed the piazza Archimede and there are soldiers outside signora Pazzi's shop to stop looting.'

'I could do with some new underwear myself. Did you get any?'

I carried on up to the second floor where Cesare lived with his mother. The door was ajar and I went into the living-room to look at the photographs again. My favourite showed a group of men standing outside a stone building. The figure nearest the camera wore the uniform of a carabiniere. The sun visor partly shaded a stern face with a handlebar moustache. Slung over his left shoulder was the shotgun we call a lupara or wolf-killer. The other man was taller with a clean shaven face entirely shaded by a panama hat. This man wore a bow tie and white shirt, jacket and riding jodhpurs with big polished boots with spurs. He was pinning a badge on the chest of the carabiniere. Below the photograph was the brass badge itself: an ear of corn between two crossed muskets. The yellowed slip of paper read, 'Presented by Prefect Mori at Roccapalumba July 1927'. Mori had signed it himself.

'Why don't you take Papa's photograph away, uncle?' came Cesare's voice from behind me. 'It means more to you than to me. After all, the two of you were old comrades. I heard you tell Flora the Tommies are bombing the clothes shops. Do they think the Sicilians will fight less well if we have no women's underwear?'

Cesare had the build of the true Sicilian: the dark colouring that comes from the Arabs who ruled the island for two hundred years, and the stockiness and barrel chest of the peasantry who toiled in the upland fields for the bread that supplied Rome. His square head with its thick hair and dark beard growth always gave me the impression that it came from an ancient Roman statue and had been plonked on his peasant shoulders so firmly that his neck had been pushed out of sight. He reminded me so strongly of his father at the same age.

'Where is your mother?'

'She's gone to the countryside to look for food. She'll be back tomorrow. Look at this.'

He handed me a paper. It was folded in the middle to make four pages striped in green white and red. I read:

'Italians! We are bombing your ports and your factories because they are working for Germany. We will bomb them until the day when Italy separates its destiny from this German war. We do not hate the Italian people...'

'Where did you get this, boy?' I asked. 'They were lying all over the street after the bombing last night,' he replied. 'Read it aloud. You know you read better than me.'

'Italians! You must believe that we have no idea of punishing you, we only hate your bosses who have humiliated Italy. Italians! You have felt the weight of our bombs. More will follow. You must choose between the peace that we offer and the destruction which the Germans and the Fascists are bringing on your city and on you. We have faith in the Italian people…'

I stopped and laughed.

'I like the bit about feeling the weight of their bombs? These are our liberators! But look what it says on the back: 'Do you want peace? If you do, demand peace. Go out and demonstrate for peace!' I didn't see many demonstrators for peace on my way over here. Now get your rifle and helmet. We're late.'

'Don't put it in your pocket, uncle. I shouldn't have shown it to you. What would happen if we were searched at the bridge?'

On the street we tied the gear to my bicycle and walked along the road to the bridge. This part of town had escaped the bombs but as we turned the corner we saw a fire engine standing outside a smouldering building. The road was covered with the ashes of documents, mixed up with dirty water. Firemen in overalls were leaning against the fire engine.

'It must have been a stray bomb,' said Cesare. 'Lucky it was a government building and not a block of flats.'

I picked up a half-charred piece of paper. We walked past the cemetery in silence, switching to the shady side of the street as the road curved away from the town. Between the road and the sea an anti-aircraft gun sat in a scoop of earth. Thick cables trailed across the dusty ground from searchlights to a truck with a portable generator.

'I wish I was with that gun crew instead of sitting out every night by the bridge,' said Cesare wistfully. 'Nothing ever happens there.'

'You aren't worried about being killed?' I replied. 'You're like the fearless young man in the fairy tale. His uncle the priest tried to scare him by locking him into the church with a supposed dead man. At midnight the dead man lifted his arms and banged the side of the coffin. 'Be quiet! I want to get some sleep!' said the fearless boy.'

'Uncle, why are you still carrying that filthy bit of paper in your hand?'

I said nothing. I was thinking of the time when I was a young man and felt no fear. We left the houses behind and walked by boarded-up workshops and bare patches of ground. In peacetime you could buy fresh vegetables from stalls on either side of the road but now food was scarce and the road was deserted. We passed corrals where sheep and goats had been kept and stables that were empty of horses.

I hummed a little tune under my breath:

' If Mori comes this way

We'll saddle up and follow;

Ride fearless all today

And fearless fight tomorrow.'

I decided to speak. 'Cesare, my fearless boy,' I said, 'do you know what building has been burned down? It was the municipal records office. All the records of births and deaths, marriages, prison records, land ownership, all were destroyed. Those firemen just turned up to make sure.'

Cesare gave me a puzzled look. 'What do you mean?' he demanded.

'The criminals know the English are coming. Yesterday a man could prove he owned a farm by going to that office and getting a copy of his deed of title. Today anybody can claim a piece of land belongs to him, and who is to say that it doesn't? Nobody knows who the criminals are any more. A man can swear that he has never gone to jail and who is to say that's a lie? It's your turn with the bicycle now.'

Cesare wheeled the bicycle along the road.

'But aren't there copies of all the documents in Rome?' he asked.

'Do you think the Tommies will send a soldier to kindly ask the Duce to look through his records? You showed me the pamphlet yourself. When the English come all our bosses will run away. The city will be governed by whomever the English choose, men who claim they have always been against Fascism. The criminals in other words but without the records the Tommies can't check. So Syracuse will be run by criminals.'

I knew what the boy was thinking. Once a policeman always a policeman, he was saying to himself. Uncle Carlo used to work for the Fascists like poor Papa did and he hates the Mafia. But who are the Mafia? Poor people like me. They wear cloth caps like me. The man who wears a hat adores the devil, that's what mother says. We've all got a little bit of Mafia in us. Manliness, courage, relying on ourselves, that's not bad.

He turned to me and tried to cheer me up.

'Never mind the criminals, uncle. It's our women we'll have to look out for when the Americans come. Do you know what people say about America? Flowers without fragrance, foods without flavour, and women without love. When they find out how loving our women are they'll stop fighting and we will all settle down together in peace.'

'But you will have to hide from the English, Cesare. The English prefer pretty boys like you to women.'

We both laughed.

3. Waterloo Bridge

Cesare was mistaken about me. I despised Mussolini just as much as I hated the Mafia. Mori had worn a black shirt when he had to, but he was a policeman first who wanted a Sicily where doors could be left open at night and where a farmer didn't have to worry about his son being kidnapped for ransom. Mussolini had got rid of Mori and let the Mafia come back. I never guessed that in a few days I would be a Mafioso myself.

The old stone bridge came into view where two rivers, the Anapo and the Ciane, run side by side just before they enter the great harbour. It is still there, a beautiful old structure. I can see it in my mind's eye as I speak to you, father. It rises in a gentle slope from the flat land by the sea and crosses the Anapo in a big arch with high parapets on either side. The level of the water was at its midsummer low and both banks were covered in rushes. On the other side of the river is an island covered with orange trees. The bridge goes over a little irrigation canal between the two streams, and by a further arch over the Ciane before the road heads up the hill towards Noto. The bridge's old name was St. Joseph's Bridge and my mother had still called it that, but its official name now was the Ponte Grande, the Big Bridge.

On the nearer end was a blockhouse and sentries guarding a barrier of concertina wire. Cesare propped the bicycle against the parapet and went inside to report for duty while I stood in the shade of a tall eucalyptus tree. I'm old enough to remember when these trees were planted all over the island to help drain the marshes. Cesare came out carrying the Breda machine gun and a box of ammunition. From dusk to dawn he and I sat in a concrete pillbox half-way between the bridge and the sea. From its slits there was a clear field of fire over the opposite bank and the little beach a hundred yards away. Cesare passed the guns and equipment down the iron steps to me. The light was fading as the sun headed towards

America.

Sicily's last day as her old self was at an end but we didn't know it. The Greeks and Romans, the Arabs, French, Spanish, and Garibaldi with his red cloak and slogans of Italy and freedom - each invader has passed over our island like a winter storm from the sea. The dust on the leaves of the eucalyptus trees is marked by a pattern of splashes of raindrops and new dust covers the pattern quickly enough. But the English and Americans were different from other invaders. They wanted nothing from the island. Our Sicily had grown used to rape but not to indifference. Somehow the evil they brought came from the fact that they never cared for us.

I have read history books in the jail but our history meant nothing to me then. I only noticed the smoke from the houses set on fire by Liberator bombers that morning. What I knew was what my mother had taught me. For her, the most ancient times were no more than 500 years back. Her poor beloved Sicily had always been at the centre of the world. In her mind, Lucifer had fallen from heaven into Etna. The Holy Family had visited Syracuse on their flight to Egypt. Of the Saracens she knew only that they were dwarves and had come after the Flood. The time of the Saracens was the time of gold and they buried many treasures in Sicily that were guarded by powerful enchantments. My mother told me when I was little that each morning when the Sultan of Turkey wakes up the first thing he does is to call his vizier and ask, 'Have the Sicilians found the treasure yet?' The vizier shakes his head and the Sultan turns to his breakfast murmuring, 'Poor, poor Sicily.'

Inside the pillbox we had a routine for the night. We told each other stories and cleaned our weapons by the light of the oil lamp until captain Valensise from the blockhouse made his inspection at midnight. Afterwards only one of us stayed on duty and the other went to sleep behind the pillbox on the side away from the bridge. That way if the captain paid another surprise inspection the sleeping man had time to wake up and pretend he had been on patrol with his rifle. We had turned out the lamp to save oil and were waiting for the captain when we heard the noise of aircraft out to sea.

Further up the road the gun was firing at the planes and we could see the flames from its muzzle and the dirty clouds shot through with yellow where the shells exploded above our heads, so we put on our steel helmets and went outside to see. Searchlights were wandering across the sky like the fingers of a blind man to find the bombers. A flash came as a stick of bombs exploded across the harbour and then after five seconds a bang and then another and another until the sounds of the guns and the roars of the bombs could no longer be distinguished apart. We stood there silently, caught up by the beauty of the fires that were reflected in the water of the harbour.

'Is this what the inside of Etna looks like?' asked Cesare. 'When the war is over I will climb to the top and look down into the crater and see if it is anything like this.'

I hoped they hadn't blown up my house.

'What power the Tommies and Amis have,' I replied.

Above me I heard a sound and I looked up.

So far I haven't talked about my father. He went to America when I was ten. One strong memory I have left of him. Early morning in the hills we had gone hunting for rabbits. The rabbits were very small and my father said they were hares but we both knew they were only rabbits. I was carrying the game bag over my shoulder with the first little rabbit in it when we turned a corner in the path. Directly ahead on an outcrop of rock was a cork tree. The leaves were beginning to turn brown for it was autumn after the first rains when the rabbits come out to feed again. An eagle that had perched on the top of the tree came gliding down towards us with its wings flapping as it tried to gain height. The brown and golden shape swished over me and I heard the same sound of the air moving as the eagle beat at it with its wings.

Later on I learned that what I was seeing above me was an English glider coming in to land but Cesare and I thought a bomber was about to crash and we hurried into the pillbox and slammed the metal door shut. Inside we bustled about to conceal our fears. Cesare counted the drums of ammunition for the Breda gun and stacked them under the slit that faced the bridge while I checked the gun's action, cocking the hammer and squeezing the trigger until the hammer fell on the empty cartridge chamber. Then I made Cesare do the same with his rifle although I thought only the Breda was any use. Suddenly there was a short burst of automatic weapons fire from the direction of the bridge and the crump of grenades exploding. We couldn't see anything in the darkness save for a glimmer of light on the river's surface. After a while I crawled through the dry riverside grass towards the bridge. As soon as I came round the parapet's edge I knew it was all wrong. There was shouting in a strange language and somebody was screaming in pain. I ran back to the pillbox, slammed the door and bolted it.

'The Tommies have taken the bridge,' I said.

'We didn't even notice.'

'Now we're completely screwed. No point in wasting ammunition just to keep up our courage.'

The first moments of tumult had passed away and time slowed down again. I could feel it dripping away in the darkness second by second but it didn't make me feel scared. The reason I'm a first-rate bodyguard isn't because I'm a good shot or have quick reactions. It's because I act calmly when there is danger around. Mori recognised that. He reasoned he was more likely to be killed by a panicky guard than a Mafia shotgun. Macaroni felt the same about me. But young Cesare was very nervous and I told him to cover the area down towards the beach. I didn't think the English would come from there but from the bridge, in short rushes like bandits. So I trained the barrel of the Breda on a bush about five yards on my side of the end of the bridge. They will have to pass in front of the bush to get nearer to my pillbox, I argued.

A rattle of automatic fire came from the bridge. I fixed my eyes on the bush and as four or five figures hurtled from behind the parapet I squeezed the trigger. But the men weren't running towards me but sideways into the roadside ditch. I should have fired a bit higher.

'The Tommies aren't after our pillbox,' I said. 'They want to cover the road from Syracuse first. Whoever is in charge knows his stuff.'

'I don't hate the Tommies, uncle.'

'Me neither. It's the evil they're bringing with them, boy. You should hate that.'

I called out again to Cesare.

'I don't think they are going to attack us right now.'

'I've fired the rifle a couple of times, Uncle Carlo, but I can't see anything.'

'Give me a drink from your water-bottle,' I said. The dawn was coming and we could see more now. A car came down the road with its headlights blazing and crashed behind the stone parapet. In the distance we heard the throbbing of diesel engines. They could be tanks, I thought. Two armoured cars came into view and I fired the Breda in short bursts at the top of the parapet. The second car blew up as I watched and the first one tried to turn around and fell into the ditch. The firing stopped again.

'Now the English will come for us,' I said.

Chips of concrete where their bullets hit the slit of the pillbox struck me in the face. I fired the Breda in short bursts as figures came from behind the parapet and two of them went down straight away.

Cesare was shouting as he fired out of the other slit. Directly in front of us the riverbank heaved up and disappeared in a cloud of earth and water, and a moment later the bunker was hit by a mortar round that blew us off our feet. The air was thick with concrete dust and the metal door was hanging loose. I stumbled up the steps and held my hands high. An English officer walked towards me with his revolver. I moved my tongue inside my mouth to make the sign of the cross as Mama had taught me to do if I ever met a devil. I expected my end.

After a moment I realised the English officer wasn't going to kill me. My brain was starting to work again. I remembered how at Gangi the doors of the other houses were opened and in each a man stood, silently watching the bandits as they were led away. Then two women, mother and daughter, threw themselves on one bandit. He was a big fat man but he staggered backwards. They were tearing at his face with their nails and pulling out his hair and screaming that he was a murderer. Murderer! Murderer! The street filled up with women. The women danced round the policemen. They were shouting with joy.

I turned around and saw them bringing Cesare's body out of the bunker.

My two Tommies were lying in the grass with their mouths open looking at me in surprise. Those two I want your forgiveness for, father. Or God's forgiveness if you wish to put it like that.

4.   Seven emeralds

Adam fell for a woman. Judas fell for thirty pieces of silver. I fell because of seven emeralds. And I didn't even get to keep them. In fact I gave them away.

The Tommies marched all the prisoners into town. On the way one of the guards stole my watch. Then we were stuck in a cave for the night. Next day the fit prisoners were set to work clearing the docks and one morning I volunteered to join a team that looked for booby traps. It might, I thought, be a way of getting back into the police force. The Germans put a lot of effort into delayed killing as they retreated. They would leave a house suitable as a billet entirely alone except for a hidden charge of explosives. The Tommies would clean up the place for use as an officers' mess and one day an officer would notice that a picture was hanging crooked. A wire led from the picture to the bomb and when he straightened the picture the bomb would go off. A few sappers started to clear our city after its liberation but the task was too big.

I liked the fact it was responsible and dangerous work. The Tommy officer with a limp told us we were making the city safe and after a few days we could all go home. Training was simple. We were given a lecture in a bad Italian that most of us found hard to understand with pictures showing where booby traps were likely to be found. Later we worked through an abandoned hotel that had been thoroughly booby-trapped with dummy bombs.

It was just like the old days when I had to search a Mafia house for guns but now it was all wires and pieces of string attached to grenades. But the work wasn't so hard and it paid well. That afternoon our truck had taken us to the square next to Castello Maniace at the tip of the island. On the other side of the square workers were pulling down the ruins of a terraced house. A man dressed in a shabby suit with a homburg hat and wearing an armband with 'Civil Authority' printed on it was watching. As we clambered out of the truck the English officer handed each prisoner a long stick and led us into the big stone building next to the gateway of the fortress. The Germans had done the work here in a rush, booby-trapping with Italian grenades. Their favourite places were where people relaxed – reaching for a bottle or closing the door of a lavatory stall. We used the rods to push on doors where the grenade might be connected to the handle and the hooks came in handy for opening cupboards or pulling on the chain of a cistern. The officer trusted me so he left me in charge with a guard on each floor and went to look for his girlfriend. The prisoners began slowly, starting at the top and going down floor by floor. They were hungry and wanted the rations and wine they had been promised at the end of the day. I had to force them on. They poked at doors, flushed toilets and pulled pictures off the walls, but nothing happened. When we had cleared all the big rooms, the tension relaxed a little. The kitchens were in the basement.

'These bastards certainly knew how to eat well,' one of the men remarked to me as we looked inside the biggest kitchen. He pushed with his stick at a pan that sat on the oak table and it clattered to the floor. A sound like a goose hissing came through the sudden silence. I jumped out of the doorway and pulled the other man with me. The explosion slammed the door to and I slowly pushed it open again. Through the dust and stench of cordite I saw that the kitchen was a wreck. The open range had fallen into the chimney. Holes in the walls showed the impact of the pans and knives that had stood on the table.

The other man looked in. 'This is a hell of a way to earn a full belly,' he whistled and left me alone to finish the job.

I carried on poking around. I hoped to find a bottle of wine and was about to leave when my eye caught the glint from a fragment of glass that had fallen out of a hole in the wall. Bending down I rummaged for an unbroken bottle. Something poured in a little dry shower over my boots and I picked up a piece. It had a green colour that reflected the light from the casement windows. I felt around carefully until seven large emerald stones lay in the palm of my hand.

After the battle at the bridge I had lost the hearing in one ear. Now I realised I was rocking from side to side and I felt light-headed so I steadied myself against the wall. My head had begun to hurt badly. I went upstairs. Outside the other prisoners were squatting in the shade of the truck and passing wine around, taking turns to chug the alcohol down their throats until the next man tugged the flask away, leaving splashes of red on the cobblestones. They looked up as I marched across the square and saluted in front of the man in the shabby suit. This was my chance, I thought, to get in at the bottom of the new administration. So I showed him the jewels and he took them from me quickly and led me back inside. We searched for more but the seven emeralds were all that had been hidden. He congratulated me and added, 'Say nothing. I will tell the Englishman that I want you to report to the mayor.'

We waited together until the officer came back and he asked permission to take me to the town hall. We set off through the streets as dusk was falling. He led and I followed. We didn't say anything to one another. When we reached the main square a man in the blue uniform of an employee of the state railways who had been sitting on the steps of the cathedral stood up and walked towards the town hall so as to meet us just a few yards away. He blocked my companion's path and brought out of his pocket a little automatic pistol.

It all happened very quickly. But instead of firing right away the man in the uniform spat and said: 'Traitor.'

Now here's a word of advice if ever you have to do a contract killing, father. Don't give the victim any warning. This man was an amateur. His delay gave me the chance to lunge forward and make a grab for the gun. It fell to the ground and he and I wrestled for a moment but he was a quick mover and he wriggled out of my grasp, grabbed his pistol from the cobbles and ran off into the gathering darkness. I lay on the ground grasping my balls where he had kicked them. To my surprise my companion didn't shout out or make any fuss. He pulled me to my feet and we hurried into the building.

That was the first time – there were several others later on – that I saved the life of Don Guiseppe Racalmuto, whom everybody at that time called vice-mayor Macaroni. He took me up to his office, poured us both big drinks of American whisky and started talking. People have always found it easy to talk to me and that evening Macaroni told me the story of his life. I think he had kept everything locked up for so long that when he started to trust somebody it all came out. Perhaps that's another reason he wants to get rid of me now. It's not just that I know too much about the Mafia. I know too much about him as a man.

The lorries with prisoners on board were heading through the square back to the quarries. Out of the window of his office we looked together at the pencil lines of light their headlamps made as they swept across the decorations of the cathedral opposite, picking the stone statues of bishops and saints out of the darkness.

'How easy it would have been to have stayed one of those prisoners,' Macaroni said to me. His biggest move had been on the day of the liberation when he turned up with his wounded colonel at the hospital. It had been full of local casualties with no space for soldiers. Like a bunch of flies buzzing around, he remembered. He had just walked right up to the doctor and told him to evacuate all his patients. Get them out - just like that. And the doctor lowered his eyes and went away and next morning all the wards were empty.

Money had flowed into Macaroni's hands from the very first day. Shops and banks wanted to reopen; farmers wanted to bring food into the city; fishermen wanted to start fishing again. Everyone needed a paper from the civil authority, and he was the man who could arrange it.

We looked at the seven green stones spread out on the desk.

'We are comrades now,' he said. 'You will be our new chief of police.' As he told me his story I realised the other possibility that he must have considered before the attempt on his life – to get rid of me. Yet later that night he told me of a Mafia principle his uncle had taught him as a boy: the only people who should be killed are your enemies who want to kill you.

Macaroni poured another drink and said he had been christened Guiseppe in the village of Racalmuto in the middle of the island. He had grown up in a house of two rooms built of gypsum rock covered over with gypsum plaster. His family had the upper room and the animals lived below. The walls were thick and cool in summer but let in the moisture from the winter rains. When it grew cold his mother filled a pan with ashes from the fire and the bread oven that stood outside the front door and Guiseppe and his brothers and sister would huddle about it wrapped in shawls. He said that one platter of wood served for the household to eat from and they all drank from a single glass.

When Guiseppe was two his eldest brother eloped with the niece of Don Toto, the biggest landowner in the village. Don Toto never forgave the family. When the Fascists took power they appointed Don Toto as commissar of the village. Racalmuto did well under Don Toto. But it was a disaster for Guiseppe's clan because Don Toto told Mori they were part of the Mafia.

One January morning little Guiseppe was awoken by banging on the door. The police were going from house to house with a list of names in their hands. His father and brothers were taken to the little square. Some of the suspects escaped but the police rounded up their livestock and held it as hostage. The square was full of bleating sheep, goats and mules all treading the falling snow into slush while the men were locked up in the police station. As the hours passed the hungry policemen had to beg for bread from the angry women of the village. Eventually the caravan of animals, prisoners and women set off in the snow for the town.

He stopped at this point and looked at me. I said: 'We were just obeying orders in those days. It was nothing personal, boss.' I had quickly slipped into the habit of calling him my boss.

The men were sent to a prison island where they broke stones for the roads. It was ten years before his father and brothers came back while his mother struggled to feed the family and his sister died. Guiseppe earned a living looking after other people's sheep and he was a handsome teenager when one day he caught the eye of a Scotswoman on her travels. They settled at her estate because the family were prepared to turn a blind eye to the gigolo provided she stayed away from the town. She was an eccentric woman like many who had lost their men in the war and she sometimes received her friends, who were mainly former VAD nurses like herself, dressed in a nightdress and riding boots. But he was caught on a visit home when Mussolini declared war and drafted into the Italian army. He avoided promotion above the rank of corporal and his war was going well until the night of liberation.

'That was the night when Guiseppe became Macaroni,' he said. 'And when I met the man who tried to kill me an hour ago.'

He and his squad were hiding in a culvert under the railway track instead of patrolling up and down the line. The bullying sergeant told him to go and discover what was happening outside. By the light of the setting moon he could see that an aircraft had crashed among the olive trees. Figures were running away. The clatter of automatic weapons started up, and then the flash of a grenade. He went back and told them an English aeroplane had landed on top of the anti-aircraft battery by the sea. The sergeant cursed and they all stayed where they were. The sounds of fighting died away but they heard boots on gravel and then a soft thud as a hand-grenade was tossed into the culvert. A deafening explosion and shooting followed. Somebody kicked him and he shouted out in English, 'Don't shoot! Don't shoot!'

He was pulled to his feet and searched. His sergeant and the others were dead or dying in the culvert. The soldiers asked him questions: Where were they? Where was the road bridge? Were there any other enemy soldiers around? They must be as scared as me, he thought. Shall I tell them we were the only Italian soldiers nearby? 'There are Italian soldiers everywhere,' he said. 'I will show you the way to the bridge.' His words were a tonic to the shaken glider troops. Their colonel was too badly wounded to walk and they did not know where they were.

'Guiseppe was the answer to their prayers. I knelt down by the wounded officer and offered to carry him on my back to the bridge.'

They walked along the track to a railway station with a goods train standing in it. He put the colonel down in a sitting position on the steps of the driver's cab and tapped some water from the boiler into a tin mug. The colonel had fainted but when he tasted the water he revived and seemed to see Guiseppe for the first time.

'He said my name was private Macaroni now,' Macaroni said to me, still looking out of the window at the darkened square which had emptied of people and vehicles.

On the other side of the goods train there was a commotion and soldiers appeared with the stationmaster. Macaroni had drunk wine with him earlier in the evening. He was shouting abuse at them. One of the soldiers butted him in the back and he fell down and they kicked him for a while but not very hard. They just wanted him to stop shouting.

'Get a door to lay me on and let's keep moving,' ordered the colonel. So the stationmaster and Macaroni carried the colonel up the line towards the bridge.

Soon they saw a wide driveway which led to an impressive house like a medieval castle with a high stone wall and serrated battlements. It was getting light and the colonel told the men they would hide up in the house for a while. Macaroni pointed at the main door and one of the soldiers shot off the lock. There was a scream of pain from inside and the soldiers kicked the door open. Macaroni slipped on a patch of blood on the threshold. In a room off the passageway a man was wriggling around like a fish on the floor. A fat woman leaned over him as she tried to staunch the bleeding from his head with her dressing gown. She looked up at Macaroni as he and the stationmaster took the colonel into the kitchen and put the stretcher on the table. Macaroni cooked an omelette on the kitchen range and boiled a kettle to make coffee. When the breakfast was ready Macaroni woke the colonel and spooned the omelette into his mouth.

Suddenly there was laughter and screams coming from the room over their heads. A teenage girl ran into the kitchen. She had thick dark hair in braids that were unravelling over her shoulders and wore a torn nightgown. Two soldiers followed after her. The stationmaster let go of the colonel's head and stood between the girl and the soldiers. Macaroni could see in the daylight that he was an older man with grey hair and a neat moustache like the king. He had his stationmaster's uniform on but underneath his jacket was his pyjama top. The two soldiers backed out of the kitchen, saying, 'This bint was hiding in the bathroom upstairs. No harm done.'

After an hour they continued up the line towards the bridge. The man who had been shot when they entered the house still lay on the floor and the girl and her mother were wailing over him as they left. The stationmaster carried his end of the door quietly. This worried Macaroni more than his earlier threats. After a few minutes there was the sound of running behind them and the two soldiers who had chased the girl downstairs caught up. At a place where the road crossed the railway they stopped to rest. A soldier came back to the main party leading a donkey cart loaded with ripe water melons striped in green and gold. The colonel on his door was loaded into the cart and they prepared to move off again. Macaroni looked around for the stationmaster and saw him hurrying back down the track towards the station.

Macaroni turned away from the window to the desk. 'That was the man who tried to kill me tonight,' he said and repeated the old Mafia maxim about only killing your enemies.

'Why have I told you this?' he asked. 'Because what has happened to Sicily in the last ten days is like an eruption of mount Etna. The lava has buried the old landscape and all the Don Totos who ran the island. But only this morning the former mayor walked in from the countryside to reclaim his office from me. He is no threat of course since he is by definition a Fascist, but the days of easy power are drawing to a close.'

We gazed at the blank space on the wall where the portrait of Mussolini had hung.

'Obviously the Duce's system has a flaw,' he went on. 'The leadership principle is dangerous if something goes wrong. It's a risky business being a leader. Mussolini won't survive the war. And after all it doesn't matter too much who is officially in charge. The mayor's deputy is more powerful than the mayor if he plays his cards right. It will never be difficult to find people who are happy to take the top jobs, receive the highest pay, wear the smartest uniforms, make the big speeches and be awarded the big medals. They will even get a big funeral if they need to be replaced.'

'No, the challenge for me is how to find trusty assistants. Sicily is beginning a new era in which the principle of the leader will be replaced by the principle of the assistant. I will do it all very quietly, not like Don Toto. I need helpers to put into all the key jobs. You are an old policeman and an honest man and you will become my chief of police. But your man job, Carlo, is to protect me from my enemies. I want you to be my bodyguard.'

So that was how I turned the corner from twenty years of serving Fascism and met private Macaroni. I pretended to myself that not much had changed. I was working for the state again, even if it was just a white armband saying 'Civil Authority.' Not everything he was doing was by the book but these were extraordinary times and together we would restore order in the city. I thought it was my duty to serve him. We slept in his office that night. The stationmaster might still be outside, I told him. As I was drifting off to sleep I thought that the emeralds didn't matter. What I could have done with them anyway. How could I have sold them? They were the problem of the vice-mayor now, my new boss.

In the hospital they give me drugs to kill the pain and sometimes I lie awake at night without pain and think: what if I had put the emeralds back in the hole? I would never have met Macaroni. And he would never have asked me to do the first murder. I was a killer by then, but I wasn't a murderer. That came a few days later.

Next morning we were disturbed by a body of peasants clumping up the marble staircase in their boots as they made their way to the mayor's office. Macaroni hurried after them and came back with a cardboard box full of identity tags from dead soldiers that he had just been given. The peasants had buried the corpses and thought handing over the ID tags would help them curry favour.

'The colonel told me to take the box away and give it to somebody,' he said. 'The colonel hates this sort of disruption.' We were still wondering what to do when a boy knocked on the door with a message that the pharmacist on the via Roma would like to see the vice-mayor.

Over a cup of real coffee in his shop the pharmacist told us his story and it made Macaroni sit up in his chair. Doctor Umberto who used to work at the hospital had called the evening before with some morphine which he wanted to swap for medicines.

'A nurse at the hospital,' said the pharmacist who held the glass phials in his hand as though they were pieces of marzipan, 'is selling Umberto this drug.'

He waited for a response. The two men had done business before. Macaroni sipped coffee and looked at the fat man in his shirtsleeves. He turned to me.

'It must be worth ten times the peacetime price now and a goldmine if we can get enough.'

The two of them agreed that the pharmacist would arrange everything. All Macaroni had to do was get Mario's restaurant open for business and turn up to meet the pharmacist there the next evening when the doctor brought in the nurse.

I left them to it and was glad to get away. Macaroni wanted me to track down the stationmaster as fast as possible. That was proper police work, not this shady business.

5.   Bella's diary

July 24th

The strange doctor has accosted me in the street outside the hospital and invited me to spend the evening with him at a puppet show. I daren't think what he wants – more drugs probably – but we need to talk. I'll put Dodo off for the night.

July 25th

We met at the puppet theatre in the heart of the old town. The cinemas have closed and this is the only entertainment. I've never seen anything like it – what fun it is! We had seats directly behind the children who occupied the first two rows. When an aged man came out with a sign that read 'The visit of Angelica to Paris' I sat forward and crossed my legs, ready to enjoy a story starring a woman. The velvet curtains on the stage parted to show the painted backdrop of a Moorish palace with minarets and palm trees. I smiled because really it wasn't very realistic, but then a puppet prince about four feet high strode on, with a dark face and spade-shaped beard, dressed entirely in black with a round silver helmet on his head.

Umberto leaned across. 'The crescent moon on the top of the helmet means he's a Saracen,' he whispered.

I was immediately drawn into the puppet world of fairytale palaces and vaulted arches. The women wear flowing robes in yellow, blue and gold and have gorgeous shoes that are absurdly too large for their tiny feet. Diamond necklaces, gold bangles and fine emerald and diamond rings are their jewels, and each one has a tiara or circlet of pearls on top of a magnificent headpiece of real hair. I found myself patting my own hair to make sure it was still there! The wooden puppets have a heart-stopping gesture of throwing out their arms and turning their hands so that they seem to be pointing straight at you. I never get tired of that.

The story was hard to follow but I didn't mind. All the magicians were at war. My sympathies were on the Moslem side because they were aided by the witch Angelica. She is taller than all the other female puppets and has a gorgeous pile of bright-red hair with a red dress and silver shoes and she carries a silver wand to use her magic on the men. I thought as I watched entranced: the stupid knights battle away with their enemies but the real war is the war between men and women. And the women are winning. Whether they are wives, mistresses or sorceresses, the women drive the plot. A kiss and a whisper in the ear of a stupid knight is all that is needed to persuade him to change sides. In the play even the emperor Charlemagne himself does pretty much what Angelica tells him. The men appear to have all the power and authority. Merlin has servants who are horned like devils and can fly through the air. But nobody is cleverer than the beautiful red-haired Angelica. She can take them on and defeat them all.

When we crossed the street for supper afterwards the restaurant was almost empty. I'm so much taller than these little Sicilians and as I moved about the little room I knocked against the glasses and cutlery on the tables. The owner Mario was as happy a man on that evening as anyone whose life revolves around cooking and serving food can be. He invited me into the kitchen and described the varieties of fish caught that day.

He began by offering me the rivetto; 'A large fish of exquisite taste, signorina.' Next to it lay the serra, the orata and the spinola. He had two varieties of sole, the linguata and the pesce luna, and a local fish called dotto or monacello, with its large prominent eyes. 'Look at the teeth of this fish,' he said. 'We call it the dentici. The flesh is as firm as that of a young chicken, lightly grilled. This here is triglia or red mullet, and these are sgombero - mackerel.' He moved to another saucepan and swept out an arm in a gesture that reminded me of the puppets. 'This pile of tiny shimmering creatures,' he announced, 'are anchovies, delicious grilled with a slice of lemon.'

I liked the look of the dotto with its great green eyes lying on the slab but I selected the palamito, which looks like the pictures of Scottish salmon I have seen in the copies of 'Country Life' in the nurses' mess.

Mario described his wines: Amarena with a flavour of cherries; Albanello; Nacarella; Occhio di Bove, made from grapes as large as bull's eyes; Capriata and Pista-Motta and above all the favourite of the English guests, Isola Bianca. So that was the one I chose, of course.

Wine and fish were served. We drank Isola Bianca and talked about puppets. The doctor explained that I have only seen a part of one of the vast play cycles about the life of Orlando, or Roland in French. He told the story of the long battles to clear Sicily of the Moslems, of the constant to and fro of the fighting. While he talked he kept glancing across the room and I noticed the other two guests looking strangely at him. He changed the subject and began describing to me the suffering of the ordinary people of the city in the weeks before the liberation, the lack of bandages and drugs and even soap to keep the wards clean.

From the doctor's lower lip hung a piece of pesce luna and I wished he would wipe it off. The wine added a tinge of pink to his sallow face. I had worked out from the start that the elaborate charade had to do with the fact that he wanted more drugs. I knew he would start talking about money soon.

'Is it possible you could do a great act of charity for the local people?' he asked. Finally, I thought, and I nodded my head. If I'm going to take the risk of stealing more morphine I want to be well rewarded. God knows what will happen when Dodo realises I am finished with him. He may try to get me kicked out of the hospital and then I will need every penny I can lay my hands on. So it was all a matter of hard negotiating. Of course everything was discussed in terms of gifts. Yes, I agreed, I would appreciate gifts, beautiful things were nice to own and they would be souvenirs which would remind me of this happy friendship. I like the way the Sicilians do business. You say one thing and mean another. It isn't very different to the Arab ways I grew up with. Afterwards he wanted to walk me back to the hostel but I said I was all right and came back here on my own. I don't want to be seen with him any more than I have to.

6.   The stationmaster

After I left Macaroni with the pharmacist I got on my bicycle and cycled the ten kilometres to Cassibile, the village where Macaroni had come across the stationmaster. I was very cautious about approaching the station building but I needn't have worried. He was nowhere to be found. The two-storey building had the number 321/004 painted on the side facing Cassibile but otherwise it looked identical to thousands of other stations all over the country. It was solidly constructed around a stone core and the windows had metal shutters and stone frames picked out in white. On the roof stood a large water tank that had been needed to fill the boilers of an older generation of locomotives. It was a great luxury to have unlimited water on an island where most people still had to walk to the well. I carried on to the village and looked up my old friend the local policeman. I found Silvio standing in the main street in his uniform but with his holster empty. We went to his house and talked over a bottle of wine in the shade with his daughter watching from the kitchen.

'I handed my gun to the Tommies on the first day,' he said, 'and watched their tanks roll up this street and knock off the end of my cousin's grocery shop. For a day or two I sat in my kitchen and moped about everything. But when my nephew ran in to say that a crowd was about to break into the shop I brushed my uniform and paraded up and down the main street, hoping that my presence would deter the people although my holster was empty.'

'How have you coped with the collapse of our beloved country, Carlo?' he asked. 'Do you love Italy as you love your home and family? I do. I think of this country as I do about my home. Now this war has been lost, I feel as though an earthquake is shaking the house. Windows and doors fly open, chimney pots hit the ground with a bang and cracks appear in the walls. In an earthquake the family inside want to run away because the house no longer protects them; instead it has become a trap that will kill them when it collapses about their ears. If the earthquake is not strong the house will survive and can be patched up again. But if the event is catastrophic the house will fall. The Tommies worship Winston Churchill because he stopped Britain falling to bits. He held the building together with his bare hands until the earthquake passed. Who will do the same for the Sicilians?'

He took another sip of wine and I waited, for I couldn't see where his story was going.

'Now our home of Italy is crashing to the ground as each brick is shaken loose from the cement. Some officials, such as a village policeman like me left on his own to keep order without a gun, try to uphold their authority. If some bricks fall intact into the rubble it means they are available to build the new Italy. Even if the new house has many private Macaronis in its foundations as well. I don't like what I hear about your new boss.'

He looked at me as though asking whether he should go on.

'Tell me about the stationmaster.'

'Vito is my friend. His wife lies next to my wife in the cemetery. Before the war life was good to us both at Cassibile.'

'Vito's life was as regular as clockwork. Early each morning I saw him standing on the platform watch in hand sniffing the acrid blend of steam and coal as the first train came in. In the evening we waited together for the last train from the city and he would turn to me and say that this daily routine was like the nerves in a body tensing up and then relaxing, as the empty milk churns were loaded back into carts and the peasants and the schoolboys and the tired clerks nodded at us as they went home. When his boys were lost in Russia and his wife died last year I worried a lot about him.'

'Where is he, Silvio?'

'I don't know. And if I did I wouldn't tell you. But try to understand. I have told you how I am coping. You are doing much the same and I'm not asking you any questions. But still no trains are running. The metal railway lines that have always shone like rays of light are dull and rusty. The platelayers have left to stay with their relatives on farms where a little food is still available. Vito has gradually sold his possessions for food. He lacks the peasant skills to tell which wayside plants are edible. So he started taking clothes in bundles on the handlebars of his bicycle to the city market. But he is a poor haggler and doesn't grasp how quickly prices are rising.'

As Silvio continued I began to understand the stationmaster. All his life he had lived under the protection of the Italian state and now he was like a helpless crab, flailing its claws after some naughty boy has flipped it on its back. He couldn't make a train run from Avola to Syracuse on his own. If the English had asked him to help he would have done so. But his brooding turned dark. How could Italy rise again, he asked Silvio, if such a man as Macaroni lived and prospered, as the rumours said he was doing in Syracuse?

'Tell me about the type of gun he has,' I asked.

'He has an automatic pistol with enough bullets. He's not a bad shot either. Your boss was lucky this time.'

7.   The English officer

Macaroni was bothered by the fact that I hadn't tracked down the stationmaster. The nurse was willing to sell drugs but not on the scale he wanted.

'Palermo's the place,' he told me. 'We can sell the morphine safely there. This business is too big for Syracuse. We need to keep doctor Umberto happy and let him have what medicines he wants. The pharmacist can handle that. But the lady needs to come through with more drugs.'

A lucky air raid broke the deadlock when German bombers sank a ship off the docks and all her papers were lost. Her name was the 'Alf P. Landon' and she was carrying medicines for the American army. It was the first time that Macaroni showed me his genius in taking advantage of an opportunity. The pharmacist had hurried over to show us a plan for dredging the drugs from the ship.

'The local lads are diving and bringing up all sorts of stuff, including morphine, as we speak. We won't have to pay that nurse,' he puffed, 'and run the risk of thieving the stuff from the hospital. It's a good idea, boss.'

The vice-mayor shook his head.

'The fishermen would only blab the story and we'd end up in jail,' he responded. 'No, I'll get the colonel upstairs to retrieve the stuff from the wreck. Then we can steal it at our leisure. The nurse won't blab. And don't call me boss. Only Carlo is allowed to call me boss.'

The English colonel who was in charge of the city signed the documents ordering the hospital to store the drugs. Macaroni had another brainwave. He decided that Umberto should pay the nurse with my emeralds. They were easier for her to hide and from Macaroni's point of view had cost him nothing. He was more concerned about how to get the drugs across the island to Palermo. The boys up there were happy to pay him in dollars for whatever he could deliver but he needed to find a secure way through the part of the island occupied by the Americans.

He and I considered various plans: taking them over the mountains on mules or using fishing boats to creep around the coast, but we still had not come up with an answer when an Englishman sauntered in to collect the shoe box the peasants had brought. The Tommy officers liked to dress eccentrically and this man was wearing a fisherman's hat with hooks stuck all over it and he had an eyepatch over one eye. He was half-way through the door on his way out and we were talking again about transport when he turned back and sitting down at the desk again he held up two dogtags and shook his head.

'I'm the king of the dead – but only in this part of the world,' he said pleasantly in bad Italian, 'and please note I just do the clearing up. Always feel Pluto gets a bad press. Anyway, this dogtag is British – Hatton D. But the oblong one is American. Quite a few Yanks in this box of yours.'

When the officer first turned to leave we had noticed a white chalk or paint line all the way down his back. Now I was mesmerised by the dogtags that swung from the damaged hand. He repeated his question.

'Where are the bodies? I have to deliver them to my American opposite number in Palermo. If I try to give him the dogtags without the bodies he is definitely going to come looking. So that's why I ask.'

Macaroni and I exchanged glances. This man was free to come and go in the American zone. A bribe might not be unacceptable. Most people find it hard to believe that somebody offering them a lot of money is all bad.

'But it is lunchtime,' Macaroni said. 'I know of a restaurant that serves fresh fish. We have excellent fish in Sicily. Do you like fish?'

Several hours later all three of us, comfortably full of monacello and anchovies with lemon all washed down with Mario's best Albanello, returned to his truck. It was a perfectly ordinary army truck except that inside it had a broad white line down the centre. The line started at the top of the windscreen in the front of the cab, separated the seating into two areas and ended at the rear tailgate. A short dark man was sitting behind the wheel on one side of the line and a tall dark man was on the other. The Englishman swept his arm across the scene like a magician revealing a trick.

'Indians,' he said. 'But there's bad news from the Raj. The Moslems are talking about a separate country for Moslems only and at my camp by the river they've painted a white line that the Hindus are not allowed to cross. Now the Hindus have painted another line down the middle of each truck. They call it a partition.'

He belched. 'It's to prevent contamination of Hindu items by non-Hindus. Or some such nonsense. At least they're not applying the rules to me. I sit with one buttock in Hindoo-stan and the other in Paki-stan. The pair of them need money since they're sending every rupee back home for their Moslem and Hindu Defence Leagues. That means they will be all right about taking your loads of ham to Palermo with the American coffins. You were talking about hams, weren't you?'

'Just hams, nothing else, I swear,' replied Macaroni.

'What's important is you can get hold of morphine for these damned pains of mine.'

He climbed aboard and sat carefully across the white line.

'That's a big problem solved,' Macaroni said afterwards. 'Now we need to look at this issue of printing advertisements for the local shops. Lieutenant Absalom is happy to split the profits from letting the local tradesmen use the printing machinery that produces his daily newspaper. The difficulty is that the military police keep stopping the carts with the bundles of advertisements. Captain Gizzard must want a share of our profits.'

'They pay no attention to my policemen. I suggest you ask the colonel for an English officer who can tell the redcaps to stick to their own rackets.'

'I'll sort that out when I can get the colonel to think about something other than his old books.'

8.   Colonel Des Demona

My plans to improve policing needed the approval of colonel Des Demona who was in charge of the city. If he agreed the next step was to ask for guns. Then I could go after the stationmaster. But we couldn't get the colonel to agree to anything. He sat upstairs all day looking at an old book he had found. It was something to do with birds, Macaroni said. He had been normal before the book and Macaroni used to take him out on tours of inspection, but now he hardly ever emerged from his rooms. The first morning after he brought the book back from the office of the head of archaeology over at the quarries he had called Macaroni upstairs to talk to him. Macaroni expected a discussion about food shortages or security but the colonel had lost interest in all those things overnight. He had the old leather book open on the table and just wanted to look out of the window:

'Kindly place my desk facing the windows.'

'Your honour wishes to look at the cathedral, no doubt.'

'No, I want to look at the air above the cathedral,' explained colonel Des. 'I am watching out for eagles.'

Macaroni worried about the colonel so one lunchtime he brought him out to have lunch with us at Mario's restaurant. This was about a week after we had sorted out the transport problem and the Englishman with the fishing hat was ferrying coffins and hams with morphine sewed into them to Palermo. The lunch suited Macaroni because he could keep an eye on his chief and at the same time slip into the kitchen and discuss the black market. He had left me alone with the colonel for a few minutes and I was chewing on pollo all'arabbiata, a specialty of the house, and watching the colonel's behaviour.

Colonel Des stopped eating every time a sparrow flew down to peck at the grains of bread under the table. The next time I looked up from my plate the Englishman fixed me with a glassy stare. He reached out his hand and picked up the carcase of the chicken from between my knife and fork.

'This is a chicken,' he said.

'It is a chicken and a very tasty one. Would you like it?'

The colonel ignored my question and lifted the bird up so that it hung between us, rotating slightly between his not very clean fingers.

'I want to see chickens - live chickens,' he replied. 'Now.'

We walked into Mario's back yard. Cases labelled 'Camp Coffee' had been unloaded from an army truck and the sergeant was enjoying a drink with Macaroni and Mario in the shade. The colonel ignored the man, who was frozen with his brandy raised halfway to his lips, and addressed Mario.

'Show me your chickens. All of them.'

Mario returned with a wicker basket. Inside were three small hens. He put it on the ground and looked expectantly at Macaroni who shrugged his shoulders.

'Open it up,' ordered colonel Des.

'Don't shake it, man!' he shouted at me. 'Let the birds come out on their own. Sergeant, give me that biscuit.'

The hens flapped out of the cage one by one and began to peck at the crumbs with little squawks and clucks. The colonel sat down on the chair and took notes while the sergeant edged away towards the truck still saluting. More biscuits were provided. Finally the hens were so full up that they refused to eat any more and made themselves comfortable under the table.

Macaroni left me to keep an eye on the colonel and when he returned from the office he found us at work dividing the activities of each hen into categories. Had it flapped its wings? Had it uttered any cries? Had it dropped the pieces of biscuit as it was eating? Above all, what sound had the biscuit made as it fell to the ground from the hen's beak? The colonel had kept telling me this was the most important question. I had tried to calm him down and an empty bottle and a saucer full of cigarette butts lay on the table.

'Sit down and listen carefully,' said the colonel. He picked up a piece of biscuit and dropped it onto the hard-packed earth of the yard.

'What sound would you say that was?'

'Tonf, sir,' replied Macaroni without hesitating.

'Tonf? I think it sounded like Boff. I'll do it again.'

'Maybe Boff this time.'

'Now I'm dropping it from a greater height.'

'Bilpo! It bounced a bit when it hit the ground.'

'You don't think it could have been Sonis?' he asked. 'Or Puls?'

'No. Perhaps Balpo. Or possibly Pilpo.'

'It's no good,' said colonel Des suddenly. 'Boff or tonf or pilpo or even balpo, they aren't Latin sounds. And no hen is tall enough to drop bread that far.'

He folded up the paper and drained his glass.

'I think I'm on the verge of a big discovery, something that will make Syracuse famous. But it's difficult to do this on my own. You've seen the problems with the chickens. I thought they would be easy compared to the eagles and the crows.'

'There are a couple of vultures near the quarries if that would help,' I said.

'Don't interrupt. What I need are the livers of freshly-killed sheep. That would be easier. The livers can't move around because they're dead.'

Macaroni led me towards the open gate where Mario watched. We agreed the Englishman was clearly a bit mad. Too many years spent digging trenches and looking for pottery during the summer heat, Macaroni said. But the best and indeed only course was to play along. If things got worse with the colonel the danger was that AMGOT would replace him. Macaroni had just heard that the Germans were pulling their troops back to the mainland. It was important to hold on to this chief while we got ready to take over from the English military. We needed to get our hands on some firearms. After all, the stationmaster might be lurking around any corner.

We walked back across the yard.

'Your chief of police will go to the slaughterhouse,' he said, 'and bring livers to your office right away.'

An hour later we gazed at the military governor of the city as he stood at his desk facing the cathedral and unwrapped three fresh raw livers wrapped in yesterday's Corriere di Siracusa.

'I'm taking you into my confidence but you must promise me that you won't reveal anything I tell you. This is very important. My book says that a liver is divided into sixteen segments and each segment is dedicated to a god.'

We promised not to tell anyone. Ash from his cigarette fell onto the livers.

'I think I'm starting to understand the Etruscan religion. You can't divide matters into important and unimportant ones. The whine of this mosquito by my ear is as meaningful as Monty's latest attack. No such thing as chance or luck exists. Understand a liver and you know what the future holds.'

He lifted his left foot and rested it on the chair so it was at right angles to his other foot on the ground.

'This is the approved position,' he said. I stole a glance at my boss and he shrugged back at me.

The Englishman held the liver in the palm of his left hand with the two large lobes hanging down like pouches and his elbow resting on his knee. The fingers of the other hand slid over the surface.

'I'm feeling for bumps.'

The sheep's liver fell to the ground with a sound that could have been Tonf! or even Boff! He wiped the dirt off with his sleeve.

'Just like the flights of birds, good fortune comes from the east or right, and bad fortune from the west or left. Now you understand how fortunate it is the Allies invaded the east of Sicily.'

His fingers slid over a bump, came back and felt it again. Taking up the second liver he felt it over for bumps or holes.

'Aha! Once again there is definitely a bump on the top right.'

As if on cue, the door opened to admit lieutenant Absalom with a copy of his newspaper.

'Latest news,' he said. 'The Jerries are evacuating across the straits to Italy, so the battle for Sicily has just been won.' After glancing at the desk and the blood stain on the floor, he hurried out.

Macaroni passed his hand over his face in despair.

The colonel looked at us in triumph as he picked up the last piece of liver.

'From the beginning I was sure that the book contains universal truth. Didn't the entrails predict good news? I'm reaching for the top right – no bump there but that is only to be expected now. But what's this?'

He held out the bloody mess towards us.

'On the part nearest my body, the southern part which belongs to Turan the love goddess? Do you think it's a bump?'

He pressed it close to his chest.

'Could it be that the goddess of love is coming my way?'

We left him clutching the liver and on the way down the stairs I asked if the colonel was asking us to find a whore for him.

'I don't think so. But he needs a woman to calm him down. Drink doesn't work, you found that out earlier. Absalom's girlfriend Nuccia will blab about the livers. The local tarts are unable to keep their mouths shut. For the colonel's girlfriend I have to find an outsider, somebody who belongs neither to Sicily nor to the Tommies, somebody we could trust. There is one possible candidate. Then we can ask the colonel to get us firearms and you can deal with the stationmaster.'

9.   Dodo

I was very happy staying on in the city and organising the clean up of all the booby traps the Jerries had left behind. I saw Bella most days and we went for walks in the old excavations. I did most of the talking. She was quieter with me than she had been in Africa.

The good times couldn't last. I was called for a medical inspection at the city hall. The doctor poked and prodded me and made me walk about the empty room while he observed me. I tried to disguise the limp but I was frightened. He could decide I was unfit for active service and ship me back home or certify me as fit and send me over to the mainland to fight for Hoppy like Lawrence was doing. The only thing I wanted was to stay in Syracuse with Bella. I left the building with the memory of the doctor's doubtful expression and as I crossed the square I saw my friend lieutenant Absalom sitting at a cafe table with the vice-mayor.

I went over and told them I was going to be reassigned. Absalom and Macaroni invited me to join them for a drink. They said there was an opening to run the police force here. The colonel in charge of the city was persuaded to make a few phone calls and I was promoted to a new role as Inspector of Police. Macaroni gave me a little Fiat as well as a grand office on the second floor of the city hall. I wasn't very busy with the local cops. Mostly my job was to keep the military police off their backs.

The following Sunday I took Bella for a special picnic. She particularly enjoyed picnics because hospital food was monotonous, and I used my police contacts to provide delicacies that were hard to get in the shops: bread rolls with a crust that you broke open to show the soft dough inside and good olive oil to pour onto it; white cheese from the milk of ewes that she said reminded her of lunches with her father at home; black and green olives; golden ripe peaches, purple figs and tangy oranges for dessert: and a bottle of the Isola Bianca. I drove the old Fiat over the bridge from Ortygia past the railway station and up the hill to the quarries. As we walked along the shady path I was talking fast and I knew my palm felt sweaty in Bella's hand as we turned a corner and stood in front of the Ear. The place was deserted now that the prisoners had gone and the tangerine trees stood with bare branches where the guards had stripped the fruit.

'If you stand outside the cave you can hear every whisper made at the back. It is a perfect place for lovers, particularly shy ones like me.'

I led her inside and left her in the darkness. Outside I nerved myself to make my declaration of love. She was very good and understanding about it to begin with and didn't want to agree to marrying me straight away. Afterwards I made a big mistake by repeating my request but she squirmed away from me, repeating the line about not being good enough, until I became angry and we both said words we didn't mean. Outside the hospital we parted in silence.

10.   Bella's diary

August 21st.

The picnic I have been looking forward to so much went all wrong. When I climbed into the car I noticed that Dodo had dressed in his full uniform and had cuts on the chin from his razor. Beads of perspiration trickled down his face. I supposed we were going back to the Greek theatre but the car stopped in front of the gate that led to the quarries. We went up to a big cave where the prisoners had been kept. It smelled of their lavatory inside.

I wondered what was going to happen. Since he hadn't brought a blanket I didn't think he would try to make love. My hand was dropped and he told me to wait in the darkness. Men always think it is so easy for a woman to wait until they do what they have decided. Why can't we take charge more often? He walked back to the entrance. I listened to the pigeons cooing softly as they flew in and out of the cave.

'Bella, I love you.'

The same words I had heard before. And now came new ones.

'I want you to marry me. Will you marry me? Will you?'

Dear diary, I'm only nineteen but I think nobody knows what path in life they will take. Sometimes in the autumn I would go walking in the fields around our town after the peasants had ploughed up the land. If the line of the path I usually walked on had been cut away by the oxen I used to peer up the slope, looking for any signs, a set of footsteps perhaps where another traveller had gone before me. But I could see nothing and so I always had to guess just where the path should be if it was to lead to the gap in the trees. And yet when I had toiled up and turned around, the path I followed without seeing it was as clear as you could wish, light against the dark of the upturned soil, and it was hard to believe I couldn't pick it out when I stood at the bottom of the hill.

So it is with events in my life. I cast about blindly but when I look back later I can see the way I took without any difficulty. That is not to say that the path I am taking is inevitable but this evening it's clear to me why I behaved as I did with Dodo.

I never began by choosing a path. I didn't want Papa to put me in the back of Dodo's truck to start with. Now though I can look back on my love affairs with Moussef and Dodo and see why I acted in a particular way. All my life I have followed my instincts. The decision I took today wasn't one that my conscious brain made for me. It happened unconsciously. Perhaps most things do.

I was touching the emeralds that I always carry for safety in my skirt pocket as he was speaking to me where I stood in the cave. Then I realised I had just said, 'No,' and I added, 'I'm sorry Dodo. I'm just not good enough for you.' I thought that would fit the bill but I had to repeat it several times before he got the message. At least, I hope he got the message. But it means I am alone.

August 23rd.

Last night I went to the grand celebration of the end of the campaign in Sicily at the town hall. The vice-mayor (whom I've got to know through doctor Umberto) organised it and made sure I got an invitation. Barbara and the other nurses were furious, especially when they saw me in the silk gown I wore for the occasion. It was probably not the right thing to show off like that but as I had the money I treated myself. I wanted Dodo to know he doesn't own me. The gown was made here in the city from parachute silk dyed the pale violet colour of Syrian hibiscus and I wore it with a pair of thin blue satin slippers. It billows out from my bare shoulders into vast sleeves. At the waist it is tightly drawn in and I wore the emerald necklace of seven stones as well.

Macaroni said he would arrange a coach to take me to the party but I thought it would be an ordinary carriage. Imagine my surprise when an old-fashioned coach in white and gold turned up at the door. It was the old state carriage of Syracuse that he had borrowed. He must have found it in a museum! Its wheels were shod in iron and on the box sat the coachman in a three-cornered hat, cracking his whip over four jet-black horses.

As I climbed in I heard one of the guards at the hostel door say, 'There goes Cinderella in her magic coach.'

When we got to the town hall the chief of police himself in his uniform held open the carriage door for me and the vice-mayor escorted me up the steps. It was all a bit like a magic ball but nothing prepared me for the surprise when he introduced me to the host of the event, the English colonel in charge of the city. We walked up the steps to where he was greeting the guests and when I saw who it was I dropped my gaze, looking down at his big shoes and the bottoms of his black trousers that barely covered his ankles. I knew without looking that he had recognized me because he stopped talking to the other guests. When I looked up I had to stop myself laughing out loud at the expression on Sticky's face! For the colonel was the same Sticky who rescued me from the puff adder at Tabarka a few weeks ago. They talk of love at first sight but from the look Sticky gave me it was more like sex at first sight! He was goggling at my cleavage and the stones with an open mouth. But he did recognise me and even remembered my name, bless him.

We started off awkwardly. Sticky spoke to me about the bird life of the city and he mentioned bird augury. I said, 'Augur. No doubt it is what the emperor Augustus, Julius Caesar's heir, took his name from?'

Sticky grabbed my arm in response and propelled me to a seat in one of the alcoves. I sat nursing the bruise while he stared out of the window muttering under his breath.

'It is all right colonel, it only hurts a little bit,' I said.

He looked at me.

'What am I dreaming of? My dear girl, here is a handkerchief. I was thinking of what you said. Of course he had to take the name of the Augustus, the one foretold by augury. His adopted father had been killed and no doubt Augustus believed his murderers intended it as a sacrifice. He was using magic to ward off the threat of another assassination. It all fits.'

He lit another cigarette.

'Finally, one wonders if that was the mistake Ovid made, the reason he was exiled?' He beamed down. 'You are a dear clever young woman. You haven't got a copy of the 'Art of Love' by any chance?'

At dinner I talked to a charming naval captain but my head was swimming with the strange things Sticky had said. When the waiters cleared away the dishes he stood up and spoke for a few minutes about peace and reconciliation. When he finished the few Sicilians in the room stood up and applauded. I noticed Umberto at the other end of the table as well as Dodo who was glowering down at his plate.

The captain steered me over to the bar and pressed me to come to the customs house steps the following afternoon where he would have a cutter waiting. Suddenly I felt my wrist being seized and Sticky was directing me away from the astonished captain across the room to the alcove. We stayed there for the rest of the evening while he told me his story. I don't think he's mad. And if he really has discovered what he thinks he has, then it is very important. I feel sure Papa would agree.

Sticky started by saying Macaroni does all the work and he spent his first days in Syracuse on tours of inspection. So he visited in grand style all the places he had known as an excavator and penniless academic. In those years he had had much trouble with the man in charge of Syracuse's antiquities. The Dottore saw his job as promoting Fascist excavations, opening up old Greek sites and demonstrating the dates had been wrongly assigned and they were in fact Roman.

On the day of liberation, Sticky said, the Dottore wore his Fascist regalia with black boots, black uniform and even the formal Ali Baba headgear with tassel. The corporal in the lead of the patrol had mistaken the swagger stick for a gun and the Dottore died with his Roman boots on. His death shook Sticky. He missed the little man. Nobody on the British side knew anything about archaeology.

'Finally I worked up the courage to ask Macaroni and paid a visit to the Dottore's headquarters. That night I couldn't sleep for excitement at what I found there.'

'What did you find?'

'On the table in the living room I picked up a large leather book written in a medieval hand. I am sure it is a complete copy of the epic poem 'Proserpine's Rape' written by the Latin poet Claudian.'

'Who?'

'The greatest poet of the late Roman era, and a mystery as well. In his thirties, prospering as a government official in Christian Rome, Claudian disappeared leaving his poem unfinished. Nobody knows what happened to him. I have the answer. He fled from Rome and settled here in Syracuse, probably in hiding for his pagan beliefs.'

'I remember Papa telling me about the poem. He said it was all to do with the hunt for Proserpine after Pluto stole her.'

'Bella dear, there isn't another person in town who knows as much as you do about the story. What a joy to meet you again. I am so happy. The unfinished version your father knew breaks off with Ceres, the mother of Proserpine, tearing up fir trees and plunging them into the crater of Etna so that she has lights to go hunting for her missing child. In the finished version I have she goes to the land of the Etruscans to find divine help and Claudian explains the old Etruscan faith and how it became the religion of Rome.'

'Why, isn't this the answer to the mystery of the cave paintings you told me about at Tabarka?' I exclaimed.

'I started reading the book directly I got back to my room. All night I read and by first light I knew that I had walked into the living world of the Etruscans. Now it is clear to me how Etruscan religion was the force behind ancient Rome. It explains the Etruscans just as well as my old idea of a Rosetta Stone. I read over and over again Claudian's account of how the Etruscans used the flight of eagles to predict the future. The next morning I got my desk moved next to the window.'

Sticky said he watched out all that day and the next for eagles without success. So he moved on to crows and ravens. Crows are a good omen and ravens are bad. The difficulty this time wasn't a lack of crows and ravens for they are plentiful in the town. But Sticky found it hard to tell them apart and furthermore both types flew in an annoyingly disorganised manner. The crow – or was it a raven? - would come into view from the right and turn around and fly away again in the direction it had come from. Sticky wasn't sure whether this counted as one good omen and one bad one. Or did they cancel out?

'I began to wonder whether Claudian had done any auguring himself or had just made it up. But I persisted with my bird-watching and refused to go on Macaroni's tours. Now though I have moved on to sheeps' livers.'

And he talked about bumps and holes in livers but by this time I was very tired. Finally he said that he would accompany me home. The old carriage lurched over the cobbles and the driver in his tricorn hat flicked his whip across the horses' backs. Sticky held my hand and I pulled him gently towards me until he could smell my perfume of attar of roses.

The horses were going round the corner at a trot and the one nearest the curb dropped to the ground. It was probably a heart attack. The chief of police told me later it is common because the animals are starving. We felt the jolt of the animal falling but for a moment the body was held by the harness and then the carriage tilted sharply to one side and the rear axle broke. We ended up together on the floor. My head was halfway out of the carriage door and Sticky was underneath me with his face pinned against my breast. I could feel that he had an erection – it was pushing up between my legs. I rearranged myself carefully on top of Sticky because I was worried that the necklace might have broken and I was determined not to move in case one of the emeralds was lost. He brushed his face against the thin silk and I heard him moaning gently. He rubbed to and fro and thrust his torso towards me. Then I think – I suspect – he came inside his dress trousers. Certainly I felt a touch of dampness when the vice-mayor and the police chief lifted me off and took us both to the hospital.

Life is so unpredictable. If the horse hadn't died Sticky would have said goodnight outside the hostel. Perhaps like the destroyer captain he would have kissed my hand. Now we both feel that something has happened to us. He is coming round tomorrow after my shift is over.

August 24th.
Sticky has had the museum opened up just for the two of us. He likes lecturing and strides from case to case in the deserted building holding forth while I trot behind, happy to be a colonel's girlfriend.

August 25th.
He visited again in his Humber limousine with the chauffeur and we drove over the hill behind the city past the tower of the Belvedere and down to the long sandy peninsula of Thapsos. I splashed around in the shallows while the sun set behind the Belvedere and Sticky swam up and down. He was trying to impress me.

August 26th.

To the beach with Sticky after work. He says that when he watches me walk back to our towels he sees a goddess rising from the waves and thinks of the story of the fisherman with whom the sea-nymph had once slept. He waited all his long life in vain to see her until one day she called out and he dived in to be with her and drown. He is so romantic!

August 28th.

We held hands in the car on the way back from the beach. It is the first time he has touched me since that night.

August 29th.

Sticky says that he is working so hard on the poem that his mind moves in the past and its myths. Sometimes he forgets not only the war but modern Sicily itself. When we have dressed and walked back to the Humber, he says, he is surprised every time by the throaty roar as the driver brings the engine to life.

August 31st.

We kissed for the first time on the way to the beach this afternoon. I hadn't washed in the morning and I'm pretty sure he hadn't either. His odour was a compound of sweat and tobacco and I'm sure there was a whiff of corned beef about me but it all added to the moment of passion in the back of the Humber. He is a lot better as a kisser than Dodo, and almost as good as dear Moussef.

11. Our Lady of Tears

You look as though you have never missed a meal in your entire life, father, if you don't mind me saying so. We have a saying that nobody is a Sicilian who hasn't missed a meal. But then you're not one of us, are you? From the north perhaps like my old boss Mori? From Bologna? I thought I recognised the accent. That's one of the reasons I trust you. You're a foreigner like he was. Another sip of water please. I'm getting to the end of my story. But first I have to tell you about the hunger.

You say you regularly fast. What happened in Sicily twenty years ago was more than the pang you feel when the bishop orders you to skip food for a day. There was real starvation around and the Tommies made the shortage of food much worse. I find it hard to forgive them for that, though I understand their reasons. They fooled themselves about what they were doing of course. The Tommies always had to believe they were being fair to us. The simple truth was that the English didn't have enough ships and they couldn't supply the army in Sicily with both food and ammunition. Ammunition came first. I could imagine the top general saying: 'There is a war on after all,' as he signed the order to take food from the locals.

Under the pressure our food rationing broke down. People who could not buy food on the black market got very hungry and small children and the elderly started to die. Mostly the elderly because fewer people cared about them.

Have you ever seen an old person who is starving to death, father? I have. Macaroni had too when he was a boy and the menfolk in his village had been locked up. We used to talk about what happens to people when they starve. The starvation of a city goes through three stages; rumour, hysteria and apathy. The final one is apathy when the slightest movement exhausts the body. That happened in Naples. Even the desire for food has gone. People lie outside their front doors or in the streets with their eyes dull and their skin drawn yellow and tight like parchment.

In Syracuse we never reached the final stage, unlike those poor bastards on the mainland. The Tommies liberated us in the height of summer after the harvest and before the vegetables could ripen under the October rains. Their army took a lot of the wheat and they forbade the fishing boats to set sail. The Tommies said the sea had to be kept clear of any craft that might be hostile. By the time the rains came the army had gone. Fishermen were able to set sail again. The wave of hunger moved onto the mainland with the Tommies. Naples starved that winter. We didn't.

Hunger built up gradually in our city before the attack because the Germans took food as well, but it got worse after the liberation. This was the time of rumours. I heard them from aunty Flora:

'The British are handing out food at the docks. Grab a bag and let's get down there as quickly as we can run!' (What my policemen found was that the pulley on a crane unloading food had broken, scattering cans in all directions and people on the spot were able to grab some corned beef. Little boys made a living for a few days diving for the tins that had gone into the harbour.)

'The grocer at the corner of via Umberto has just got flour in. Macaroni has told him to sell it at the old price. Hurry up!' (I told Flora this was true but as soon as the shopkeeper had satisfied his regular customers he closed the shutters. The rest he traded for Camp coffee which Mario was buying from the British. The crowd waited outside all night on the chance he had some left. When he opened up the next morning only a few of them could afford his coffee.)

'D'you see these plants with five leaves on each stem sitting in the pan on the stove? I don't know what they're called – I'm a fisherman's wife not a peasant – but they are growing in the fields. If you soak them for twelve hours they are good to eat, or so my cousin says.' (The plants brought on stomach pains and vomiting and were poisonous if given to small children. It didn't matter how long you soaked them for.)

People adjusted to the shortage of food. Many women slept with the British and got presents of food or cigarettes they could trade for food.

Hunger's second stage grew out of the rumours. People who are hungry see things or witness strange events, visions or miracles. You know that, father, even though you won't say so out loud. I witnessed a miracle myself in those days. In fact you might even say I made up another one as well.

A few months ago I walked into the new concrete shrine of Our Lady of Tears that dominates the upper part of our beloved town, looking like an umbrella thrust two hundred feet into the sky. I found it almost empty. At the entrance I didn't even see any beggars, which is a sure sign that visitors are few and far between. The only people inside were the woman who sells souvenirs and the burly man who cleans the floors. There was no scent of religious piety and not even any candles burning in front of the altar with the famous little plaque. The only smell was a clean lemony tang and it came from the floor polish. It struck me that like many people from humble origins who have done well (and at the time I included myself) the little Madonna looked a bit lost in her big house, which is surprisingly close to via Giardino down the hill where she started from in 1943.

I had moved into Cesare's old flat after Macaroni hired me. Cesare's mother hadn't come back and nobody knew what had happened to her. Staying there meant I could share the extra food I got as a policeman with aunty Flora, the old lady who lived downstairs. Flora tried hard to pretend that not a lot had changed since the liberation. She treasured the odd stroke of fortune as when an English nurse had thrown cigarettes at her. She chatted to her neighbours as before.

Now her clients were young women and the clothes she ironed were flowery summer dresses and silk slips. She was learning to take payment in British and American cigarettes and what was the right exchange rate. One Chesterfield was worth two Bengal Lancers, she told me. One evening when I was talking to her as she was doing the ironing a girl came in to collect her lingerie and laid on the table some banknotes that Flora had never seen.

'This is the American money I got from my new boyfriend. Look, even the writing is in American. Allied Military Currency. Issued in Italy. One Lira.'

The young woman read it slowly to us, proud of her ability to pronounce a few words.

'What about our own money with the king on it, Nuccia?'

'You have to move with the times, aunty. That's all finished. We're part of America now.'

After I took up residence she told me she had been walking out of town and bringing back wild grasses and vegetables to cook for her supper. Sometimes she ate them raw like an animal as she picked them. Flora wasn't hungry all the time now that I was around but she was still affected by the feeling of hysteria that grew in the city as the weeks of liberation drew on.

'Have you heard about the statue of the Madonna on via Giardino?' she asked one evening as we were sharing a bowl of pasta. 'She is weeping tears, real tears for our sufferings.'

I lifted the plate to my mouth and answered, 'No, but I heard yesterday that when the priest at Floridia was saying mass the statue of Christ above the altar moved one of his arms and blessed the holy bread.'

I looked at her face with its little mouth open wide to show the few teeth she had left and finished licking my plate clean.

'What I say is that the Saviour needs to give us more bread instead of just blessing the little we've got.'

'Carlo, you shouldn't laugh at miracles. They are signs of God's compassion for our sufferings.'

'Things must be really bad if those fat-cat priests are seeing things too.'

I agreed to go with her to via Giardino. As we got near the road began to fill up with people hurrying in the same direction and I took Flora by the arm. In the square several of Gizzard's jeeps were parked in front of the photographer's shop on the corner and the road that led to the docks had been blocked off with concertina wire. Around us the pushing and jostling grew more violent and we moved to the fringes of the crowd and went up via Statella. The rich of Syracuse once had their gardens and orchards here with a view of the harbour. At the corner we could see the house below where via Pasubio meets via Giardino.

Like all the houses in the mean streets by the port where the fishermen lived number 21 was a single-storey building painted a dirty yellow. The door and the window beside were closed and shuttered. It looked like a house under siege. I felt myself being drawn towards it as though the stones under my feet had begun to slide downwards of their own accord. The house became larger. I wasn't aware that I was moving but I put Flora in front to shield her from the pressure of the crowd.

Everybody was shouting, 'Little Madonna, little Madonna, come out and bless us.'

People around us wept and held handkerchiefs up to their faces. Men hoisted children onto their shoulders so they could see better and I lifted Flora off the ground as well. She cried out with the others for the Madonnina to come out and save her. When I tried to put her down again there was no space for her feet so I held on to her, but now I couldn't see the house any more. The sun had set and darkness was spreading like a blanket over the crowd. I was jabbed in the ribs as the man next to me lifted his arms free to light a candle and pass it up to a little girl perched on his shoulders. Around me the flames of candles were wavering above the heads and shoulders of the people, the men with bare heads and the women all wearing black scarves. The window shutters tweaked open and a scared face peered out.

I'm a Sicilian and Sicilians believe that you can't make a solid distinction between the everyday world and what you see in your dreams. Dreams are a warning of what will happen to you and they can also comment on what has happened in the past and give it meaning. We swear that in the final moments before you go to sleep and just before you wake up, you cross the boundary from one world to the other and you can belong to both. In some families there is a skill passed down from mother to children of controlling what happens in your dreams by coming awake inside the dream. But we are practical people and the real point of the skill is to question the departed. It may be that this is how the soothsayers and prophesiers who used to be so important on our island gained their reputation.

My mother tried to teach me the skill but I wasn't good at recalling what happened in my dreams. One dawn though when I was a young man out on the hills hunting bandits, I woke up and remembered that I had come awake inside my dream and seen my dead grandmother walk into the family kitchen where I spent the first years of my life.

'Nonna, what is it like when you die?' I asked her. She sat by the fireside as usual and looked down at me, the flames dancing in her eyes.

'Carlo my boy, it's what happens afterwards that matters,' she replied.

As I rolled over in my damp blankets I had a deep feeling of satisfaction from her response. She had said in the simplest way that the after-life was real and more significant that anything on Sicily. I have never told anybody about this before you, father, and I don't think of it as a vision. It certainly didn't make me go to mass except on the feast of Saint Lucy and it is years since I have confessed to a priest. Now in front of the house at via Giardino I felt I was in another waking dream and that if I shouted as loudly as everybody else in the crowd, that frightened face in the window would be replaced by the statue of the Madonnina glinting in the light of hundreds of candles.

The pressure on my chest was so tight that I could hardly breathe but I managed to get the air out of my lungs and shout with the others. Just then the little girl on her father's shoulders started to scream. She was wearing an elaborate white dress with petticoats that must have been made for her first communion. The candle had touched the flimsy tulle material and set it alight. She disappeared from view as her father dropped her and his neighbours tried to get their hands free so they could beat out the flames. The smell of burning cloth filled the air and the spell was broken.

When I had pushed out of the crowd, walking backwards and not caring if I knocked people over, I carried Flora home and put her to bed. Her dress was torn and as I covered her up with a sheet I saw the bruising on the thin body. Upstairs I lay down to wait for morning but I couldn't sleep and at dawn I went back to via Giardino. Even before I reached the square nearby I could hear the crowd chanting for the little Madonna and when I got to the top of the street I saw there were more people than ever in front of number 21. Heavy with the dust of Africa a wind was blowing in from the sea and I had to shield my eyes with my hand. Seeing there was no chance of getting into the house I walked over the bridge to Ortygia so I could talk to Macaroni.

12. The plaque of the little Madonna

He had just returned from Palermo and held a leather satchel on his lap as he listened to me.

'The crowd are going mad and shouting for the statue to be brought out so they can touch it. My neighbour came away with bruises all over her body. Somebody is going to get killed if we don't do something.'

'What about the redcaps?'

'The English are sitting in their jeeps in the square but all they do is keep the crowd off the main street to the docks. They aren't Christians like us.'

'Did you see the little Madonna yourself?' asked Macaroni. 'It's a wall plaque by the way, not a statue. Mary holding out her bleeding heart, that type of thing. Well, now this woman is far gone in pregnancy and what with the shortage of food and worry she completely lost her sight and took to bed. Two nights ago she opened her eyes and cried she could see again thanks to the Madonna. When they looked at the plaque real tears were dripping down.'

We crossed ourselves.

'Get some of your men together and we'll go there, Carlo. But I can't believe it's as bad as you say.'

In the square Macaroni lit up a Lucky Strike. Suddenly he shot out an arm to detain a man who was hurriedly walking past the building.

'Where are you off to in such a hurry, doctor?'

'I'm on my way home from the hospital.'

'Come along with us to see the little Madonna. We might need some medical assistance and I see you've got your bag with you.'

Umberto turned out to be the key to getting through the crowd because he was well-liked and people made way for him. Even so it wasn't easy to get into number 21. The mood of the crowd was different each time. Yesterday it had been more peaceful but now the people in the streets were hungry and thirsty and they wanted badly to see the little Madonna. The wind had got up further.

Inside the front room the place stank of sweat and the noise from the crowd made it hard to hear what anybody was saying. A woman appeared from the bedroom and ushered us to a bureau under the window. She took out something covered with a white cloth, laid it on the bureau and carefully lifted away the cloth. The heat was stifling and people were jammed together peering over each other's shoulders. I saw an ordinary majolica image of the Virgin in blue and white on a backing of black glass. She was holding a bleeding heart. But the room was dark so without thinking I leaned across and opened a shutter.

Instantly the wind slammed both shutters wide and a score of hands reached in like tentacles from the street, pulling at the iron frame over the window. I tried to step back but the others pushed towards the bureau, ignoring the sightless waving hands and the redoubled chanting from outside. The plaque had become wet. But we had no time to take this in before there was a snapping sound as the iron frame came away from its sockets. I jumped to the window and punched at the figures trying to climb in. One man was already on the windowsill but I hit him square in the face and heard a crack as the jawbone broke. The body of a little girl was thrown through the window into the room but then we managed to bolt tight the shutters.

The chanting outside had turned into one word, repeated over and over: 'Maddonina, Madonnina.'

I put my mouth next to Macaroni's ear.

'If they break in we'll be torn to pieces. Our only chance is to show them the little Madonna. It might calm them down.'

We both looked around at the faces frozen with a mixture of awe at the miracle of the tears and shock at the noise. The shutters were vibrating under the blows of countless fists. They won't hold for long, I thought. The women were on their knees and the figure on the bed was in a trance, staring at the ceiling with her mouth open. I held the little girl in my arms and comforted her. She had one hand in her mouth and I noticed that the other arm hung limply. She's paralysed, I guessed. They tossed her in so the Madonnina can cure her. That gave me an idea.

I gestured to Macaroni and Umberto to come closer. 'Boss,' I bellowed, 'I'm going to open the front door and clear the veranda with my men. You take hold of the little girl and do what I say.'

Umberto's face was as white as the robe of the Madonnina. Macaroni grabbed the man's arm and gave him the satchel.

'Take my bag and don't let it go under any circumstances.'

Then he picked up the little girl and held her as though she was a riot shield.

I flung the front door wide and the policemen charged down the steps with linked arms. Taking the plaque from the bureau I quickly stepped out. The force of the wind pushed me to one side but I steadied myself and held the plaque up high so everybody could see it.

'See the little Madonna! Kneel and pray for the Madonnina to perform a miracle!'

Only the people in the front row had the space to kneel. The rest inclined their heads and the atmosphere of violence dissipated a little. I continued to shout.

'See the little girl. This little girl is praying to the little Madonna to be made well again. Pray with her. Pray, people of Syracuse.'

From the crowd arose a vast whispering sound. To those of us in danger on the veranda it seemed as though a thousand snakes were slithering around our shoes.

'Now the little child will touch the Madonna with her withered arm.'

Macaroni lifted the little girl up towards the plaque so she touched it with her paralysed hand. Immediately I called out, 'A miracle, a miracle!

The little girl can move her arm! Thank you, holy Madonna!'

The crowd fell silent and waited for the next miracle to occur. Now was the moment to leave. Doctor Umberto appeared in the doorway. I suddenly realised the flaw in my plan. I was still holding the plaque.

An individual at the foot of the steps stood up. He had a neatly-trimmed moustache and wore the red cap and blue uniform of an employee of the state railways. What the stationmaster was doing there nobody will ever know. Perhaps he had meant to go straight to the town hall that morning to kill Macaroni but had been drawn by the crowds to number 21. He pointed his pistol at Macaroni, who held out the girl in front of him. The stationmaster tried to move to one side so that he didn't hit the girl but he tripped over a kneeling woman and the gun went off. Doctor Umberto was slammed against the front door and fell down. A large red mess appeared on the wood of the door. Macaroni and I dashed back inside.

The plaque felt slippy in my hands so I put it on the table. Macaroni was cursing and trying to open the door again. I restrained him.

'Get the bag!' he screamed.

Together we opened the door. The gunman had gone. Doctor Umberto lay dead still with one of my policemen bending over him. The satchel was open beside the body and all the dollars from Palermo were swirling around in the dust storm. Macaroni picked a ten dollar bill off the front of his suit. A woman in a black dress and scarf was scrabbling at the bank notes that had become stuck to the mess of blood, leather and broken glass on the veranda. She lifted her hands full of money to the sky.

'Another miracle!' she cried. 'The little Madonna has sent us money from heaven!'

By the time the British jeeps reached via Giardino most of the crowd had dispersed. Macaroni and I headed for the city hall right away. A few lucky people left with dollars but most only with the impression of having witnessed the miracle of the girl's healing. Some shops were broken into and food taken. The banknotes were blown into the harbour by the wind and the fishermen put out their nets on the surface of the water and brought back a rich catch. For months afterwards the little boys of our city went out on hunts 'to find the rest of the Doctor's money', combing the alleyways and climbing on every rooftop in the area. Nobody handed the money back. Gizzard's redcaps did pick up some, together with the remains of the dumdum bullet they dug out of the front door and what was left of the satchel and the medicine bag.

Meanwhile we were trying to stay one step ahead. We told the Tommy captain who had been seconded to us that the killer was the stationmaster from Cassibile and that the city police must be in charge of the investigation, not the redcaps. The dead man was a local and it was no concern of theirs. Then before he disappeared for Palermo Macaroni spoke to the officer who was moving the morphine with the coffins and asked him if he knew a way to hold things up for forty-eight hours.

Gizzard arrested everybody in the house except the Madonnina as well as people in the street outside who had not run away. The Tommy and I went over to his cells to listen to the interrogations and I realised right away the redcaps wouldn't get very far. He was questioning the father of the little girl with the withered arm.

'What can you tell us about the killing of doctor Umberto?'

'Doctor Umberto has been murdered? Where?'

'Outside number 21 via Giardino. We picked you up there.'

'Yes I admit that, but my girl had just been healed by the little Madonna. I was hugging her to me in joy and praying. And now you say the good doctor was killed! I can't understand why I didn't notice anything.'

Gizzard found penicillin ampoules in the doctor's medicine bag. This was a complete surprise to me as I had no idea the nurse was selling anything other than morphine. He asked the matron at the hospital to come over to his office and when she arrived I knew from one glance at her face that we were all in deep trouble. She had discovered of course that it wasn't just a few ampoules of penicillin that had gone. The entire supply of morphine from the 'Alf P. Landon' had vanished.

'It has to be that African girl,' she said. 'All my other girls are trustworthy, even the ones who are sleeping with Poticare. But that African girl, her with the fancy makeup and trying to twist the dear colonel around her finger, it has to be her. She must have been selling the morphine. I'll never be promoted now.'

She fingered the fragments of morphine bottles on the desk.

'But what can you expect from a kike?'

The Tommy officer swept his hat off the desk and headed out of the room. He managed to stay ahead of me all the way to the car.

13.   Bella's diary

September 13th.

This has been the worst day of my life. I should never have given the doctor any of the penicillin that has just arrived. It bothered me all night and I was woken up by a knock on the door of my room. When I opened I saw two Indian soldiers, one tall and one short. The short one saluted and said that his major needed to talk to me about stealing drugs. The tall one smiled knowingly and held the door so I couldn't close it. They gave me a minute to pack a bag and then marched me out of the building and put me in the back of a truck with a white line down the middle. I felt as though I was having a nightmare.

They have brought me here to an army camp by a large pool of water somewhere outside the city. The land is flat with a stream winding through it and reeds and bulrushes grow thickly on either side. We crossed the stream by a big stone bridge and they turned off the road and followed a series of tracks until as the light was fading the truck halted by the pool. I was startled to hear the call to prayer for the first time since I left Africa. In a funny way it was very comforting.

'La illaha illa Allah. There is no God but Allah.'

The man waiting to meet me was the same horrible officer with one eye who played the TF Bundy trick on Dodo. He introduced himself as Scuffy Lintle and pretended to be very pleasant but he made sure there was no chance for me to run away.

'That's the Moslem contingent,' the man said. 'Watch out for this line of white stones. Our mutual friend the vice-mayor has told me the story, by the way, and asked me to keep you safe for a while. Drugs are missing and you and the doctor who was killed...Yes it happened this morning... are mixed up in it.'

He put me in a tent close to the pool with a guard outside. I lay on the camp bed for a few minutes with my hands over my face before I undressed and began to wash. Suddenly I heard a creak from the bed and turned around. Scuffy Lintle was sitting there, still wearing his tweed hat festooned with fishing flies. He shook his head as I stood with one arm across my breasts and the other between my thighs, and the black threads in front of his face moved as though there was a cobweb curtain between the two of us. He flipped up the patch so that I saw his blind milky eye sitting in the middle of its pool of angry red flesh.

I grabbed for the towel and held it in front of me as though he was a bull in the ring and I was a bullfighter. He continued to shake his head.

'You don't need to worry about me, Miss Bella. Looking and staring is all I'm good for now. And moving about so nobody can hear me. You see this?'

He held up a hand with a finger gone.

'It's not the only digit I've got missing. I stepped on an S-mine at Alamein. Much as I would love to wrestle you onto this bed, there wouldn't be any point.'

As he talked in this disgusting manner he turned my clothes inside out and patted them, running his fingers along the seams.

'You haven't brought any pharmaceuticals? We're running short of morphine in camp and the British only have Omnipon. If you let the good doctor have drugs to help his patients, why not? The Americans have got bags of the real stuff to hand out, I hear. If we're giving penicillin to soldiers who've got the clap from sleeping with the local whores – pardon my French – why shouldn't he have some to save a dying baby? And if you've been stealing morphine – good luck, everybody's doing it. '

I started to protest.

'Don't say anything, my dear. I've told you I don't care. You can stay here as long as you want. Meanwhile, your water is getting cold. Supper in half an hour - the curry will be something special, I promise you.'

Supper was laid out beneath a canopy of aspen leaves that shone black and silver in the light of the oil lamp. Scuffy served the food and drink. He wouldn't stop talking.

'I'm camped here for the fishing,' he explained, 'but I read in the evenings sometimes. This pool was where Pluto came after he'd seized Proserpine. He needed to find a way back home with his bride. In they went, Pluto, Proserpine, chariot and all.'

'So this pool is an entrance to the underworld?'

'There are many roads to hell, Miss Bella. I learned them at boarding school. Here at Fonte Ciane, mount Etna itself, Lake Pergusa, Lake Gurrida, the Palici. Thirteen on Sicily alone. Can I pour you another whisky?'

'No thanks.'

'There's at least one in Turkey, four in Greece including a cave at Matapan where we whipped the Eyeties a couple of years back, and a spot near Naples. I'll look that one up when I'm in Italy.'

He refilled his mug with Johnny Walker.

'The fish comes from the pool. I caught it this morning, a big fat red mullet.'

We both ate the curry.

'Do you believe in hell? It's more likely than heaven I think.'

'What did the Romans think of hell?' I asked, happy to keep the conversation away from pharmaceuticals.

'A dead-end for most. But for some a place like Blackpool or Monte Carlo which you could visit and come back alive. There was even love down there. Let's be the first tourists in hell, you and me. We'll try all those gateways until we find one that's still open. Here, have another spoonful of sergeant Madass's curry.'

He has left me alone now but I worry that he is spying on me. There are peepholes in the canvas.

September 14th.

When I walked out of the tent this morning I saw a large object floating on the surface of the pool. At first I thought it was a kitbag but then I realised what it was and I couldn't stop screaming. Scuffy hurried up and led me back inside. Sitting on the unmade camp bed he explained it all to me. He is an expert on the dead. The troops in the gliders carried lots of kit so if their gliders were shot down and they fell into the water their bodies sank to the bottom. He stroked my hand quite gently.

'When the webbing rots the body floats free and comes to the surface.'

'But the fish must have been feeding on that…that thing! And I ate your fish curry last night!' I began to retch.

He left me there to get his troops organised to drag the body downwind of my tent. I haven't gone outside all day. I can't get out of my head the image of that huge belly and the mouth wide open in a grin, as though it was proud at having come up from hell and scared a young girl.

I pray constantly for Dodo or Sticky to come and rescue me.

14.   Dodo

One of the strangest things down here is that everybody sees what they want to see. It took me a long time to realise and most people never do because they don't stay long enough -they are just passing through. Take what happened this morning as an example. I was on my way to the Gate and I suppose I was lost in my own dreams because as I was crossing the road in front of the tube station I heard a screeching of brakes behind me and I was knocked to the ground. I picked myself up and rubbed the dirt off my knees. A beefy sergeant climbed down from the cab of his fifteen hundredweight truck and marched towards me.

'Why don't you look where you're going? I nearly killed you,' he bellowed.

I said I was sorry but he cursed again and said I had made him late for work.

'You've messed up your suit, and I've got a scratch on my new car,' he complained as he rubbed the metal bumper of the truck.

Because I understand how things work here, I asked him about his vehicle and he described something quite different to the truck, even as he had his hand on the bonnet. For him it was bright silver, not a camouflage green colour, and it had alloy wheels and other things I can't make head or tail of. Looking at him I saw a sergeant in Royal Engineer overalls with grease stains and a black beret. But he wasn't. He was a businessman who was late for work.

Once you realise this it can be scary. What do I look like to him? Obviously I'm not a captain in the Indian army wearing my summer kit of tunic and shorts. Am I another businessman? When I buy tea for a squaddy at the Naafi, what does he see when he looks round? I see a linoleum floor, plain deal tables with ashtrays and soldiers lining up at the counter for egg and chips. Where does he think he is? When Bella comes – and she will come – what will I look like to her, and she to me? But I have faith in my love.

On the last day of my life I went as usual to the city hall to report for duty. A local civilian had been killed. The vice-mayor told me to go over to Gizzard's and stop him taking control of the murder inquiry. The killer was a railway official from Cassibile, he said, and it was nothing to do with the redcaps. When I learned from matron Hamilton that Bella might be involved I tried to find her at the hospital. But she wasn't at the pharmacy or on the wards and when I reached her hostel, Gizzard had got there before me. He was enjoying himself. As a detective-sergeant in the West End before the war he thought he knew all about the links between drugs, girls and crime. Now that a pretty nurse was missing, he told me, together with a considerable amount of cash and morphine he was confident that prostitution would fit into the Umberto affair in due course.

I stood in the corridor outside the little room and watched as the captain and his men poured out the contents of the chest of drawers onto the bed, rifled through the brushes and toiletries and finally slit open the mattress. Gizzard let out a squeak of delight and tipped the emeralds out of a cloth bag into his palm.

'And how could a poor auxiliary nurse have acquired this finery?' he asked.

I came into the room and sat down beside him on the bed, staring at the back of the door on which hung the silk gown the colour of hibiscus.

Gizzard answered his own question.

'From selling drugs of course. Unless she was engaging in prostitution. Probably she was doing both. She is French, I understand.'

'Bella Imago, a French citizen,' I said steadily. 'She joined the Queen Alexandra's in Tunisia earlier this year. She told me she was nineteen years old, but that may be false. In fact I'm not even sure of her real name.'

'We know all that.' Gizzard was triumphant.

I was already hurrying along the corridor. I must rescue Bella, I thought. Get the killer first and question him to find out where she is. On the street I ordered the police chief to drive me to the station at Cassibile and took the box of bullets out of my pocket to load the gun.

The car went round a corner and I saw Bella walking away down an alley. I got out and ran after her, but when I reached her the face was different and I let the startled woman go. Walking back to the vehicle I remembered my dream. I had been playing cricket against the Nizam of Hyderabad and instead of scoring a century the umpire had given me out. All the fielders were women wrapped in black cloaks and I demanded to see which one had the ball. I pulled the cloak off the first woman but underneath was Scuffy Lintle looking at me with his bad eye. Behind him I knew the women were tossing the ball from one to another so I would never find which one had caught me out.

I reached the car and told the policeman to drive on. I rubbed the scar on my temple. My head hurt.

The station looked deserted when we walked over from the parked car, a creepy sort of place with grass growing up between the stones of the platform. I pushed the door open and shouted but there was no answer. The downstairs room on the right must have served as a mess room for the men who maintained the rails, with benches and wooden chests for their tools. Opposite was the office where the stationmaster had issued tickets. In the middle stood a large oak desk with eight drawers and the telephone and the old telegraph apparatus. Everything was covered with a mixture of dust and the red sand from Africa blown in by the storm.

I told the policeman to wait and I took the service revolver out of its holster and walked up the stairs to the living area on the first floor. Upstairs was a family bathroom and a kitchen and bedroom. The bed had recently been slept in. A metal door led to the veranda with a view beyond the orange groves to the blue line of the sea. A man was sitting there now looking stupidly at me. On the table was a bottle of wine, a glass and a gun. I pointed my revolver at the man.

That's all. I don't recall anything more. There's nothing else, like the spool of film after it has run through the projector going round and round. I found myself on the tube, hanging on to the strap with a lot of Japanese soldiers as the train pulled into the Gate. Peter met me outside on the street and took me off to his mess for a large gin and tonic.

15.   Confession

The English officer had been upstairs only a minute when I heard the gunshot and shouted but there was no response so I ran back to the car. The Tommies were still the only ones allowed to carry a firearm. That's when I saw them. I have been a killer, father, but I have never thought about suicide. It's a mortal sin. So when I saw the box of cartridges lying on the floor I was shocked. The captain must have left them in the car before he went into the building with an unloaded gun. The suspect was armed, I had told him that. He was upset about the nurse but I had no idea he would go so far. When I heard later how she had dumped him a couple of weeks before and he was due to go back to England, it made sense. After all, he had sat with his head in his hands all through the journey.

As I was leaning in with the door open looking at the sealed box I saw out of the corner of my eye the stationmaster running up the tracks away from the building. After waiting a couple of minutes I went back inside and found the captain's body on the veranda. His empty revolver was in his hand. I loaded the gun and followed. I didn't have to go far. The stationmaster was waiting for me about half a mile up the track, sitting on a pile of railway sleepers with his gun beside him. As soon as he saw me he moved away from the gun and began to talk. A lot of stuff about his childhood to begin with, coming to Sicily as a boy on a winter's morning forty years before and how he had never forgotten his first view of the station at Syracuse. He talked as though I wasn't there, remembering the sulphur districts where the dry land was the colour of yellow sulphur and his mother fed the pig on prickly pears. When his father's monthly pay ran out he was sent into the countryside to find wild snails and chicory to eat.

'I'm hungry now,' he said. 'But you'll give me something to eat at the jail, and a cup of coffee perhaps. I haven't tasted coffee for ever so long.

This way is better than shooting the bastard. I can ruin him instead. Take the pistol. I'm not going to fight. I only shot the Tommy because he pulled the trigger first, but he had something wrong with his gun.'

I motioned him back down the railway line to the station and he went willingly. Every so often he turned around and talked at me. It was as though he was addressing a courtroom.

'When I got back to the station the first morning I walked into my office. It was a wreck. The place stank of urine. I lifted the telephone to call Syracuse but the line was dead. The cables for the telephone and telegraph had been ripped out of the wall. Upstairs I poured out wine from the bottle and thought of the men with whom I had been drinking the evening before. One of them, the corporal I had just seen helping the British, was a traitor.'

He walked on for a minute and then said something about a girl being raped and left for dead.

We reached my car and he turned around and held his hands out so I could handcuff them. I didn't have any handcuffs so we just stood there in silence for a moment.

'I'm looking forward to my trial,' he said. 'I've been doing a lot of digging about your boss and there's dirt enough. The pharmacist at Noto is ready to give evidence. He knows what your boss has been doing with all the morphine you stole from the Americans. His brother-in-law wants to take over as mayor of Syracuse. I have many allies, men who detest what is being done to this country in the name of collaboration...'

He went on making speeches to the imaginary courtroom, but I wasn't listening. Instead I was thinking of my life before I met Macaroni. Mornings spent hanging around the docks looking for a night's work on a fishing boat. Lies to the landlady about where the next week's rent was coming from. Afternoons standing in the street markets selling my mementoes for the price of a bowl of soup. Above all I remembered being hungry and ashamed. Today I was the chief of police with honour, good pay and authority. What did it matter if some morphine and penicillin had been stolen? Nobody had been hurt. The only person who had killed anyone was the figure in front of me. He had shot doctor Umberto, a good man, and was mixed up in the death of the Tommy captain. Did I want to go back to what I had been before the liberation? I was doing good works now, restoring law and order by putting policemen on the streets. Soon the Tommies would hand things over to us. We would get our guns back. I looked down at the revolver in my hand.

I don't need to go on, do I father? You get the picture. This is what I wanted to confess. After the first murder there is no other. I could tell you about the pharmacist who went quietly to begin with and squealed like a pig at the end, or Silvio my friend whom I shot in the back because I didn't dare look him in the face, and the other killings down the years. I am sorry for these sins and all the sins I can't remember. Now give me my penance.

First a sip of coffee from your cup? Bless you, father. Raise my head so I don't spill any.

Ugh! how foul it tastes. How it burns my throat! Don't force me to drink. Stop, I pray you.

16.   Bella's diary

September 15th.

Dodo is dead. That is the first thing to write down. Next, I am still a prisoner.

The vice-mayor came to Scuffy's camp in a fine big saloon car flying an American flag from its bonnet. With him was an enormous bald general who filled up the back seat so I had to sit in the front. Macaroni wouldn't say anything to me on the way into town. When we stopped in front of the city hall and I looked up at Sticky's windows, I was horrified to see him leaning right out and thought he might topple over. He saw us and waved and then he pointed at the sky. In his office we found him talking to captain Gizzard over a mess of livers and newspapers on his desk.

'I don't see the point of all this,' Sticky was saying. 'The killer has been shot resisting arrest after carrying out a second murder, this time of captain Deeds.'

I gasped and Macaroni held me upright.

'I have already explained to you colonel, that the theft of drugs from the hospital, the presence of thousands of dollars at the crime scene and the murders are all linked. And the key person is this nurse who had the jewellery and serves in a supporting arm of His Majesty's armed forces. I'm glad to see the vice-mayor is handing her over to the authorities.'

That was me, I supposed. My emeralds were lying on Sticky's desk.

Sticky stood up and walked over to Macaroni. At me he just glanced briefly.

'Botelli's eagles,' he said quietly. 'Rare birds. They flew into view from the right and circled over the cathedral just as you arrived. I'm relying on you.'

The American came puffing into the office and overflowed the antique armchair that Macaroni pulled out for him. He introduced himself and announced he was taking over the whole of the second floor for his investigation of the murders and thefts.

'How many of you are there?' Sticky asked.

'Seventeen. An NYPD detective with fluent Sicilian who will question witnesses and conduct inquiries. A Navy captain who will search the wreck of the 'Alf P. Landon' for any remaining stores. A colonel in the Air Force for aerial photography – though to be honest we just brought him along to keep our access to the Dakotas – and a professor from John Hopkins who is an expert on penicillin and opiates and can help us determine the extent of salt water damage to the cargo. A lawyer from the Department of Justice in Washington DC who will act as my chief of staff. A loading specialist. Lady stenographers. Printers and mimeographers. Security personnel. Drivers. Could be more than seventeen.'

A silence followed and Gizzard said uncertainly: 'But this is my investigation. I already have a culprit and a motive for the theft of the drugs and the murder. How did the French nurse come by these emeralds if not by crime?'

I moved across the room and stood behind the general. He seemed more interested in the rococo chair than in what the captain had to say. He ran his large fingers over the worn plush arms.

Now Sticky did a very brave and loving thing. He picked up an emerald and began polishing the stone with a handkerchief.

'I gave these jewels to Miss Imago,' he said, 'as a gift. We are engaged to be married.'

I nodded in agreement.

'Well in that case,' Gizzard said in a bullying defiant tone, 'of course I shall still continue my enquiries. What is clear is that Umberto had thousands of dollars and stolen drugs on him when he was killed.'

Macaroni coughed. All the while the others talked he had been doodling on a piece of paper: dollar signs, arrows, hearts and question marks all connected by squiggles.

'You speak of facts but there is no evidence connecting the doctor with any thefts. Only the penicillin was found on him and he could have bought that elsewhere. The money was his own, I am sure. If the crowd in via Giardino learn we are accusing the good doctor of being a criminal there will be further riots.'

They looked at him blankly, save for the general who was now at the window examining the curtains.

'Why was he killed then?'

'Captain, the doctor was defending the little Madonna. I was there. Meanwhile the urgent task is to stop the rioting.'

'Go ahead and explain yourself,' responded Sticky. 'I for one am listening,' he added, looking at Gizzard. I noticed that he was transferring the rest of the emeralds from the desk to his handkerchief.

Later Scuffy brought me back to his camp.

September 16th.

Last night they put Macaroni's plan into action. The local police guarded the Madonna as she left via Giardino. They took her to the nearby square where a service of intercession for the city's suffering was held. Thousands of local people wearing black armbands as a sign of mourning for the doctor followed the plaque. Several miracles occurred as the image passed through the streets but Scuffy just laughs and won't let me know what they are. The bishop prayed for the soul of the doctor before handing the microphone to Sticky. He announced that local patients would be admitted to the hospital where they would receive the best care and all medicines including penicillin. The hospital had been renamed 'Doctor Umberto Hospital'.

September 17th.
Macaroni was right. There were no riots in the city yesterday or today.

September 18th.
The general has begun his investigation. The naval captain sailed around the sunken wreck and has done some fishing with Scuffy. No sign of the Air Force colonel as yet.

September 19th.
Scuffy came back from the hospital drunk – so drunk that he forgot to collect the bodies and Madass had to go back for them. Poticare told him the American professor made a nuisance of himself until he was invited to help remove a gall bladder, after which they have become friends and do ward rounds together. Poticare says the professor knows nothing about penicillin or morphine and has no idea why he is in Syracuse.

It's all very odd. They haven't asked to speak to me yet.

September 20th.
Absalom turned up this morning. I thought he had come to take me to be interrogated. But he had two ladies in the jeep with him. I've not seen American ladies before. They are a pair of blondes with matching Betty Grable coiffures. Scuffy says they work as stenographers for the general and bathe every morning in identical red swimsuits from the steps by the fountain of Arethusa. Scuffy's theory is that Absalom is trying to prise them apart so he can pursue one or the other. He wanted a bottle of whisky and they went off to the Belvedere for a picnic.

September 21st.
Scuffy broke the news to me. Dodo let himself be shot. He committed suicide. If only I had understood how much he loved me I might have

saved him!

September 22nd
I am still mourning for Dodo.

September 23rd.
No news. Still mourning. Chicken curry in the evening.

September 24th.
The enormous general and his senior detective work long hours in the office on the second floor with its rococo furniture, according to Scuffy. They only open the door to request coffee. At night they sit up late eating Mario's cooking and drinking his best wines. Macaroni is exhausted keeping up with them. This has gone on for six days.

September 25th.
Absalom has been ordered out of the room with the printing equipment. The office is sealed while the report is prepared and copied. He drove down here and complained to Scuffy he hadn't got anywhere with the blondes. I hope everyone has forgotten about me and I can go back to the hospital.

September 26th.
Scuffy drove me to the city hall. He said I was free. I went upstairs to see Sticky and found him with Macaroni and the matron, talking to the general who was walking around the room admiring the furnishings.

'The murderer was identified and killed by your local police force while attempting to evade arrest. That side of the business is clear,' the general said. 'As for the penicillin found at the crime scene, checking at the hospital we discovered errors in record-keeping and it is unlikely that any penicillin was in fact taken. We incline to your vice-mayor's view that the victim obtained it elsewhere with his own money.'

Sticky turned to matron Hamilton who nodded.

'I checked the records again before leaving to take charge of Queen Alexandra's nurses in Italy.'

'The most important matter,' wheezed the general as he examined the pictures on the walls, 'is the supposed theft of morphine and between ourselves it's the real reason I was asked to take this case. Well, nothing was stolen because there was nothing to steal. The 'Alf P. Landon' was not carrying pharmaceuticals. We've checked with the port authorities in Baltimore and there's no record of any drugs being loaded.'

He pointed to a landscape painting and added, 'Very fine.'

'Still we've had a pleasant stay,' he concluded, 'and that guy Mario sure knows how to cook. Have you got your copies of the report to hand?'

He scooped them into his briefcase and wagged a finger at Sticky who was sitting with his mouth open while Macaroni looked out of the window.

'My advice is to put a lid on this whole thing. I don't know what you Brits took out of the 'Alf P. Landon' but it sure wasn't pharmaceuticals and I suggest you adjust your records accordingly. You've got a really fine place here, by the way.'

They all left and I gave Sticky a big kiss. He said I couldn't go back to the hospital and I said it didn't matter. I sat in one of the armchairs and he got down on one knee and asked me to marry him. He says Macaroni can marry us as he is taking over as mayor. Sticky has been ordered back to England.

I will still be a refugee, even on the boat that takes us to his home. Only nineteen years old and what experiences I have had! Moussef treated me well. I behaved badly with dear Dodo and he let himself be killed because of me. How can I ever forgive myself for his death? Sticky says he will be famous when his book is published and I will be his consort. It is time to settle down after all that has happened. I am sure I can be happy with him. I will make tea for his students and go along to his lectures. Perhaps we will have a child and I will name him after Papa.

And if it doesn't work out with Sticky I still have the emeralds, and my own courage. Yes, I have my courage.

So he walked me down the staircase to have a coffee in the square and decide where I was to stay before the wedding. On the second floor we stopped. The door to the rooms the Americans had used was open and we looked inside. Now we know what they needed the Dakotas for. The general and his team have stripped the second floor. The antique furniture, Baroque mirrors, Venetian crystal candelabra dating back to the time of the Bourbon kings, rococo desks and armchairs– even the red plush armchair on which Garibaldi sat – all are gone. The panelled walls have dark square patches where paintings once hung and the sunlight streams in through the tall windows, now bare of the heavy silk curtains that graced them.

Absalom was gazing around.

'You've got to hand it to the Yanks,' he said in admiration.

17.   Bella's diary (the present day)

July 9th.

The limousine from the airport dropped me off at the hotel last night so
I had no opportunity to see Syracuse. I was really tired and slept until
midday. When I pulled back the curtains I was nearly blinded by the
sunlight. I had forgotten about the Sicilian sunlight. After lunch I went on
a stroll through the city. Not much of a walk because I have to stop and
rest every hundred yards or so. My heart is pounding and I feel dizzy.
What do the bystanders think when they see a little old widow with grey
hair and a walking stick, bending over and coughing at a street corner?
And I don't remember much, I realise. The cathedral and the city hall,
they haven't changed. But the hospital has been completely rebuilt. It is
unrecognisable.

The streets are full of dark faces, immigrants from Africa. I watched a
story on the television about refugees who survived in the water for days
by clinging to the buoys of a fishing line. The local people hate them, you
can see that in their faces. I suppose they hated me all those years ago.
But now that I can stay in the best hotel and wear fine clothes they
respect me. It is very strange to look about you and think that you are one
of only a few people who remember the war and the liberation. But then
I remind myself that I didn't come here to see the sights and admire the
city. I don't give a damn about the city. I have hired a car and driver to
take me to the place tomorrow.

July 10th.

Dodo is buried in a war graves cemetery on the main road to Augusta.
Once upon a time it must have been in the countryside but now it is
surrounded by industrial sites. A car showroom stands across the road
and the ditch by the gateway is full of litter. Trucks roar by and my driver
had to park around the corner. The white gravestones are neatly ranked in

rows and as you walk up the slope from the gate (resting as I have to do) they form different patterns. At the top there is a huge grey stone cross with a metal sword set into it.

I found the place where he is buried eventually and laid down the bunch of flowers I bought by the cathedral this morning. It is so strange to think that he is still only twenty-four years old. Standing there I thought: The army took the men under this soil from their individual lives and made out of them a collective being. They drilled on chilly barracks squares. In the evenings they drank beer and went to the cinema and chased girls together. They shared the same hopes and fears, endured a common fate and in the end they were reunited. They lie just as far apart as if Scuffy had ordered them to stand with each man touching his neighbour's shoulder with his outstretched arm and fall backwards into the earth.

July 11th.

I had a bad attack last night, the worst yet. It was hard even to get out of bed but I have dressed and am waiting to go to the cemetery. The emeralds are in my pocket. I will kneel down and take two handfuls of soil. If I pray very hard perhaps he will come. I am scared: what will he want with an old woman when he is only twenty-four? Still, I believe there is love even in hell. Reach up and take me.

THE END

www.ingramcontent.com/pod-product-compliance
Lightning Source LLC
Chambersburg PA
CBHW050527260626
47157CB00004B/1498